*Learn to Say Goodbye*

# Learn to say goodbye

## DOLORES WARWICK

*An Ariel Book*
*Farrar, Straus & Giroux*
*New York*

*For Mirzi, with love*

*Learn to Say Goodbye*

# Chapter 1

It was the end of a long winter and everything looked dirty to Lucy. The sky was muddied with bleak threats of more rain. The trees waved thin black branches against the evening air. Even the cars that inched their way along through the five-o'clock traffic were speckled with grime and streaked with melted snow. Lucy saw the bus lumber over the hill, its headlights glowing. She reached for her carfare and her fingers found the two holes in the pocket of her coat. Somehow, that filled her with an unaccountable sense of anger, and she fished viciously in the other pocket among lipstick, comb, and the forbidden cigarettes until she found the proper change. The bus hissed to a stop and she climbed on, dropped her fare into the box, and slid gratefully into a seat by the window.

For the first few blocks Lucy concerned herself only with the lighted houses the bus was passing. It was easier that way at first. But somewhere between here and St. Michael's Home she would have to think about the afternoon at home with her mother, decide what she would tell the girls and what she would keep to herself, think up some of the elaborate inventions they always exchanged after seeing their families. No one was ever really fooled. It was a terrible way to live.

Cautiously, a little at a time, Lucy allowed herself to remember how it had begun. At school she had borrowed money from Carol for a package of cigarettes.

"Sister Christine will kill you."

"She won't know—I want them for this afternoon; I'm going to see my mother."

"Oh, okay."

After Typing III, her last class, she had hurried to her locker for her things. Down at the end of the locker room Helen, Joanne, and Ginny were throwing books in their lockers, banging doors, talking too loudly. They always acted that way at school and Lucy hated it. She hated having to get on the same bus with them to ride back to the Home, hated the curious stares of passengers when the group of five high-school girls gathered up their things and got off at the big gray stone building on Summit Street where the enormous statue of Christ waited with outstretched arms to welcome them.

Lucy and Carol usually found a seat together at the back of the bus and pretended they didn't know the other three. Last year they had started getting off two blocks ahead of their stop and walking the rest of the way home. It was a way of pretending that they were no part of it all. But the other three had gone to Sister Christine with injured airs and made such a case out of it that Sister had called Lucy and Carol into her office for "Lecture Number One" as they called it, about group loyalties, public impressions, being mature, and all the rest of it. They had been forced to abandon the small comfort of their fantasy. Lucy was glad that at least today she'd be able to ride home alone and anonymous.

The ride from Western High to Franklin Street, where her mother lived, was a short one. Lucy would have walked, but Sister Christine had given her extra money for carfare, saying that that way she could save time and have a longer visit. Lucy knew that Sister meant that she didn't want her walking in that neighborhood, even for seven blocks in broad daylight. It had made her angry with Sister, angry with her mother for living here, angry with herself for having to think, once again, about the problems of having two "homes" and two "mothers."

Her mother was in the kitchen making coffee when Lucy came in. The house had the same smell she always remembered: a combination of expensive perfume, stale cigarette smoke, and coffee brewing.

"Hello, Mamma, it's me."

"Lucy honey, I'll be out to you in a minute, I'm just putting on a pot of coffee. I didn't even have a chance to tidy up, I don't know where the time flew to. I've been waiting all week to see you this afternoon, and here you are and I haven't even had a chance to freshen up."

Lucy had taken the chair by the window as she always did, listened to the monologue of apologies that never varied when she visited, and examined the room as she waited for her mother to pad in from the kitchen in soft-soled bedroom slippers. The rooms seemed smaller each time she came back, but she'd decided that was because the rooms at St. Michael's were so enormous. Here, in her mother's house, you could sit on the sofa and, if you stretched out your legs, you could almost touch the feet of the person sitting in the armchair by the window. The pink cabbage roses that had once bloomed all over the rug now showed only in a pale, faded clump at the center. The overstuffed red sofa where Lucy's mother would soon come and sit was covered with magazines, newspapers, and a slight shedding of white hairs from Dandy, the huge Persian cat that sat looking unblinkingly at Lucy.

Across the room, the fireplace that no longer burned anything shouldered an oversized marble mantelpiece. Here Lucy liked most to linger, feasting on the clutter of fine china and porcelain that always seemed to be trying to tell her something about who and what she was. She walked over to the mantelpiece and looked at the fine blue tracery against clean white on the Meissen bowls, the sturdier blue and white of the Delft shoe and the tiny open-toed slipper that she dimly remembered sipping medicine from, the Belleek vase with pale thistles stemming up along each side, the squat mugs of ruby glass circled by a band of thumbprints, the crystal decanters that shot prismatic darts of color against the tan and brown diamonds of the wallpaper—they all suggested something faraway and fine that wasn't like Mamma, or like Lucy either. They were like the things of someone you wish you knew but would be afraid to talk to. And yet they always managed to make Lucy feel homesick for something. Once, holding the Delft

*6*

shoe, she had gotten a tight, still feeling in her mind that tried to grow into a memory. She had closed her eyes, to allow it to take shape. There was something about a baby holding the shoe in its fist and someone laughing and saying she could wear it if they had the match. The baby must have been Marcella, her younger sister. But before her mind could gather enough edges to hold onto, the scene spread out, dimly liquid and formless, as it always did each time Lucy tried to remember what it had been like before she lived at the Home.

Surely she was not homesick for this ugly little house on Franklin Street where Mamma lived—in a maroon chenille bathrobe and slippers most of the time—or even for Mamma, with her strange remarks, long silences while she stared into her amber-colored glass of ginger ale that, for a long time now, Lucy had known wasn't ginger ale. Mamma and her silent tears that began unpredictably, collected around the huge black frames of the glasses that made her myopic eyes seem larger than they really were, and finally slipped off the rims of the glasses and into the hollow wells above her cheekbones that seemed specially designed to collect Mamma's kind of tears. Lucy didn't know if she loved her or not. But she did know that this wasn't what her heart was hunting after when she got that sick, sad feeling that was almost a comfort each time she looked at the things on the mantelpiece.

And she wasn't, could never be, homesick for St. Michael's. In a way, she supposed, the Home was home. One hundred years ago it had been called St. Michael's Home for Orphaned and Destitute Children. You could still read that in the cornerstone if you climbed behind the barberry hedge massed thickly against the east wall of the building. But hardly anyone did that any more. It was as though someone had planned the torn clothing and scratched faces and arms as punishment for those who wanted to remember that long ago there had been real orphan girls here. They were girls for whom the Home was a haven, a shelter of conventual care, warm clothing, nourishing food, and a kind of maternal love from the starched bosoms of nuns who cared for the children-without-parents that the world could not care for.

The honest faces of those honest orphans could be discovered all over the house even now, sometimes sad but always serene, in their identical white middy blouses with dark ties and dark skirts. There were photographs of them in the big Bishop's Parlor on the first floor, where the nuns spoke softly with visiting clergy and the girls spoke to social workers, from the uncomfortable edges of carved Victorian furniture. Sister Gratia had photographs of them hanging, improbably, in the huge basement kitchen, collecting a greasy film from fried chicken for fifty-seven girls. Every so often, old Sister Gratia would climb stiffly onto a chair and wipe the glass clean with one edge of her long white apron, then lift the other edge to dab first at her eyes, then at her upper lip beaded with perspiration. "Lovely girls, my darlings they were," she would murmur, more to herself than to the current crop of girls assigned to help in the kitchen or dishroom. "We had a fine set of girls here in those days." No one liked working in the kitchen with Sister Gratia.

"Well, times sure have changed, Sister," someone was always certain to say when the old nuns began their futile fetching of examples from the past. "Those girls probably loved you like a mother, but I've got a mother, see? Some of us have even got two, and well, three's a crowd, Sister."

Sister Gratia and the older nuns never adjusted to these deliberately flippant words. Sister Marian and the younger nuns would make an equally flip reply or glance darkly, which meant "Watch your manner, young lady," depending on how far you had gone or how they felt that particular minute. It didn't really matter much either way. None of the nuns knew how it was. The ones who tried to find out were worse than the ones who let you alone. It was usually the young ones who wanted to "understand," which was the latest word for *nosy* as far as Lucy was concerned. And yet some of them were so pretty, or so sweet when they forgot about trying to be, or simply good. You'd meet one of them coming around the corner from the chapel, and before she knew you were there you got a look at her face. Good was all you could call it, because some of them were certainly not pretty, but there was something clean and strong, but soft at the same time, that outlined the curve of their lips or the shape of their eyes. And it made you stand quiet so you could get another second or two to look at her before she caught sight of you there in the corridor and smiled and rumpled your hair or some other silly thing. If it *was* goodness, pure and simple, then Sister Christine was probably right about how attractive it was in a human being. Whatever it was, it was the closest Lucy ever came to loving any of them. You had to love someone or you'd die.

But those moments were infrequent enough. Most of the time you just hated the Home and the nuns, hated your parents and the girls there, who were your only friends and who knew too much about you to be your friends for long. You ended up hating yourself a lot of the time.

Her mother came into the living room then, and Lucy sat down in the chair by the window, leaving the mantelpiece with a feeling something like guilt. If you made the mistake of letting Mamma see you looking at those things too long, she'd tell you for two hours what a fine family yours used to be or else tell you that, whatever else you did, you must never get married, because that was the end of everything. Lucy couldn't believe either was really true, but she never knew what to say.

"I've made you a pot of coffee, unless you'd rather have ginger ale," her mother said, carrying her own glass to the table beside the sofa and putting a plastic cup and saucer on the arm of Lucy's chair.

"Coffee's fine. Sister never lets us have it," Lucy said. "She never lets us have these either," she added, pulling out the package of cigarettes and lighting one clumsily.

"You'll have enough of everything to last you a lifetime when the Sisters aren't arranging your life," her mother said. Lucy didn't know whether the bitterness was directed toward the Sisters or toward life. "Did Sister give you that skirt?"

"What's the matter with it?"

"Well, it looks sort of pinned-together to me."

"Mamma, it's a kilt—you know, Scotch." Lucy already hated the skirt.

"How's school?"

"Okay, I guess. Those girls are a bunch of creeps. All of them think they're going to be somebody's private secretary and none of them will ever do anything but work in some moldy old office. At least I know that's where I'll end up, so I'm not going to be disappointed."

"Did you know penicillin grows in mold?" her mother asked.

"Now what has that got to do with business school? Honestly, Mamma, I wish you'd listen to me."

"Lucy honey, I listened to you crying for six straight months after you were born, and you told me everything about yourself then. Tell me something about Marcella. Now there's a baby that never told me a thing. All I know about that one I learn from the social workers."

Her mother pulled nervously on the tail of the Persian cat beside her and took a long, thirsty-looking swallow from her drink.

"Mamma, how can you stand to have that horrible old cat around you all the time? He's always shedding." Lucy took a last inexpert puff on the cigarette and crushed it viciously in the saucer rimmed with dark-brown coffee stains. She hated black coffee, and Mamma never brought sugar or cream with it.

"How do you expect me to tell you anything about Marcella? I don't go to school with her, I don't go to dinner with her, I don't go to chapel with her, I don't go to bed with her. I'm not her mother, you know." It all came out in a rush, a tangled string of angry words that somehow made her ready to cry.

"Forget it, honey, forget it. If you can't forgive it, just forget it. That's my motto. I'll have that painted on your coat of arms for a wedding present."

Impulsively, her mother stood up and took the three steps required to cross the tiny room. She knelt on the rug full of cabbage roses and tried to put her arm around Lucy's shoulder, but somehow it ended up with her head on Lucy's lap, and Lucy was patting Mamma's shoulder as if she were a baby and telling her not to cry.

"Lucy honey," she said, "when you were a baby you loved your Mamma, and now you know her. When you grow up, try to forgive her."

"Sure, Mamma, and Marcella's fine. She's building a doll's village out of Popsicle sticks and it's really great. She's got houses, and a hotel, a church, a bus station—she says there's going to be a theater with an actual stage as soon as she collects enough sticks. The kids tell her she's crazy, but they all save the sticks for her and everybody stops off at her dormitory every day to see if there's anything new."

Her mother got up suddenly and began dancing around the room; not a here-we-go-round-the-mulberry-bush kind of dance, but a slow, graceful dance that was as formal as a minuet. You expected to see the shabby old bathrobe and slippers turn into a satin gown with shoes to match and to see a powdered wig piled high with curls appear on her head. Her face was faraway too; it was as if she had stepped out of a picture before they had a chance to finish painting on the proper costume and facial expression. Lucy watched, fascinated and half frightened, for you never knew what Mamma might do when she got like this. And yet it was beautiful to see her so sure of where she was going, so confident that what she was doing was right. She danced that way for a full two minutes, finishing with a deep curtsy to the mantelpiece.

"Mamma, where did you learn to dance like that?"

Her mother didn't answer. She stood looking at her reflection in the ugly gilt-framed mirror that hung over the fireplace. Then she flattened the palm of her hand and swept the Delft shoe onto the floor as though it were a suddenly discovered spider.

"You didn't think I could do that, did you?" she asked, turning to Lucy.

"Mamma, why?"

"Why? Because I went to Miss Ogilvy's Dancing Forum for seven years, that's why. We learned every dance the world has ever known," she finished dully, and went back to the red sofa, where she hugged Dandy between sips of her drink until the cat scratched his way out of her arms and came over to rub himself against Lucy's legs. Lucy stood up quickly, hating the feel of his fur. "I'll sweep that up for you, Mamma," she said, and went to the kitchen for the broom and dustpan that stood beside the door. She felt dizzy and slightly sick. She swept up the pieces of china, carried them back to the kitchen, and placed them carefully inside the sleeve of her green sweater. Then she knocked the dustpan against the wastebasket to make a sound like dumping something. She came back to the living room and picked up her coat from the back of the chair, where she had laid it when she came in.

"Mamma, I'm sorry I can't stay any longer, but it takes me almost an hour to get home and I'm on kitchen duty this week, so I have to be there by five." It was a lie, but it didn't bother her nearly as much as the edges of china that were scraping against the inside of her arm, and she hurried into her coat and picked up her books to disguise the shape of her left sleeve.

"It was hardly worth the carfare down here, was it?" her mother asked. "And how long do the experts decide we should wait between visits—it's once a month for a home visit these days, isn't it?"

"Oh, Mamma, you can come out to the Home any weekend, you know that."

"Why, of course I can, and we can sit on one of those comfortable stone benches in the front yard and watch the kids without visitors come by picking their noses, with their eyes as big as saucers. Or we can go whisper in the corner of a television lounge with three other families whispering in three other corners, and everybody paying more attention to what's going on in the other corners than what's going on in his own. Or we can visit in the Bishop's Parlor, and have a nun swoop in every five minutes and say, 'Oh, excuse me, Mrs. Brannan, I thought Father Farrell was in here!' No, thanks, honey, I'd rather see you here." She stood up and swirled the last rim of liquid around in the bottom of her glass before drinking it. "I'm going to have another. Are you sure you won't stay and have a last cup of coffee with your mother?"

"No, thanks, Mamma, really, I've got to get back."

"Well, we'll talk about your boyfriends the next time you come. That's what mothers talk to their teenage daughters about, isn't it?"

Lucy felt ready to cry, but Mamma laughed then, a wonderful, happy laugh that belonged to green parks with children feeding swans on the lake and a carousel tooting calliope music into a blue summer sky. The laugh affected Lucy like an event, and she laughed too as she hugged her mother with one arm and bent down her cheek for the ritual kiss.

She held onto the laugh all the way down the block to the bus stop, but the twenty-minute wait and the darkening sky infected her like a contagion, and by the time she finally found her seat on the bus she couldn't have smiled if the city had suddenly turned into a Technicolor circus. It was as dark as the middle of night when she stepped off the bus at the Summit Street corner, even though it was only a little after five o'clock. Christ loomed ominously on the front lawn and only the familiarity of lighted windows dotting the dark stone façade of the building made the walk up the front drive anything short of frightening. The huge trees so magnificent by day were full of dark secrets by night. Lucy hurried past them as the wind stung her cheeks. She rang the big brass bell at the front door, and in the space of its echoing inside, and the time it would take someone on door duty to come down and answer it, she fingered the pieces of Delft now in her pocket. She'd glue that shoe back together again if it took her a year.

The door opened and it was Carol.

"Hi. Got a cigarette?" she whispered. Lucy tried to laugh with her but only managed a tired grin.

"I'll be up in a minute, I'm going to stop in the chapel first," she said.

"Oh? Was it that bad, or have you suddenly got religion?"

"Don't be funny, I'm not in the mood," Lucy answered crossly, and walked away from the hurt expression on the face of her best friend.

The Sisters were finishing evening prayers when Lucy slipped quietly into the last pew and sat down. The sight of them all together there, heads covered with identical black, prayer books on the seats behind them as they knelt, was as familiar and reassuring as anything Lucy could think of at the moment. She hadn't come there to pray but to readjust from the home on Franklin Street to the one on Summit Street. The sound of their voices as they prayed aloud was comforting as a lullaby, and she closed her eyes until a last Amen, more resounding than the others, roused her. Lucy slipped out of the back pew and left the chapel without genuflecting.

# Chapter 2

Lucy could hear them arguing louder than the sound of the radio when she was only halfway upstairs. "What a bunch of bigmouths," she thought, hurrying a little. At the top of the steps the hall ran for ten feet before the three broad stairs that led into the dormitory. Lucy paused at the end of the hall, enjoying the shock of familiarity for a moment.

"Here's the world traveler, safely returned to her happy home," said Ginny. "How was your mother?"

"Lucy hasn't got a mother; she has a mamma." Joanne deliberately drawled the last word, making it sound like the voice of a doll that wet when you gave it a bottle of water.

"I guess a mamma is better than a nightclub dancer that won't let you call her anything but Charlene," Lucy retorted furiously.

"At least Joanne's mother works for a living," said Helen. "What *does* your mother do all day, Lucy? Aside from filling prescriptions. That *is* medicine she takes every hour, isn't it?"

Rage, cold yet blazing, directed Lucy's hand to Helen's face. The slap was loud enough to sound clearly at the other end of the room, where Carol was lying on her bed reading a magazine. She looked up for an instant before turning the next page.

"You're going to be sorry for that, Brannan." Helen spoke softly; her usually fair skin had gone milky white. Not once did she even touch her fingers to her cheek, although Lucy could see four thin lines of red drawn across the blanched skin, and four small spots directly beneath them. Lucy's breath was fluttering strangely in her throat, and she swallowed twice over a bad taste in her mouth. Her own face, ordinarily sallow in tone, burned with two bright spots of color high above the cheekbones. She crossed the length of the dormitory, the sound of her scuffed loafers loud and distorted against the polished oak flooring.

Why did it always have to begin like that, she wondered. And end like that. Everything turned into a battle. She snapped on the reading lamp on the desk beside her bed, unloaded the books from her arm, took off her coat, and hung it up. Then she sat down at her desk and opened a book, staring blindly at the print that was blurring in watery waves.

In a minute the bell would ring and dinner on a metal

cart would be rolled into the dining room by two kitchen assistants from the ancient elevator that whirred, grumbled, and clanked its way complainingly up the shaft. There would be at least a minor quarrel as to who should unload the cart, followed by another about unfair portions of favorite foods. Sister Marian would appear in the doorway of the dining room toward the end of the meal and look hurt at the recital of grievances hurled at her for immediate judgment. It was enough to make anybody feel like quarreling.

"I'm getting seasick from the brain waves around here," Joanne said. Lucy ignored the remark and turned a page.

"Study hard, become a good secretary, and you may marry the boss. Mrs. Lucy Bigboss. Will you have us all over for tea when you're Mrs. Bigboss? I can see it now. 'Hello, girls. Do come in and have some tea. Remember the good old days at St. Michael's? Those were the happiest days of my life. Such fun we had.'"

Joanne lounged on her bed across the room, filing her nails absently. She was a plain girl, with the sort of nondescript looks that always reminded people of someone they knew, yet never made enough of an impression to let them remember Joanne. She spent a great deal of her time trying to give herself a more memorable look. Her eyes were small and narrower than average, so that her face seemed slightly feline, a look she encouraged by applying quantities of mascara, eye liner, and eyebrow pencil. Joanne's hair color was lost somewhere between blond and brown; she tried to discover it periodically with alternate treatments of platinum and chestnut rinses. On school nights she spent most of the study period from seven to ten arranging her hair in perpetually changing styles. Joanne's desk was filled with bottles, jars, and tubes of cosmetics that she guarded as though they held a magic formula for success to the person who happened on the proper combination of ingredients. Joanne pursued the subject with fierce determination. Meanwhile, she contented herself with cruelly accurate mimicry that seemed suited to her indefinite appearance; her face and voice could meet the demands of any impersonation. Now, curled on her bed, she was busy with the nail file, looking like a cat serenely sharpening its claws.

The bell rang for dinner then. Lucy closed the book and stood up. She waited to see how they would group themselves for dinner. There were two tables in the dining room, and Sister Marian let them arrange the seating as they pleased. On rare occasions, the five girls would crowd together around one table. Usually, Lucy and Carol sat at one, obviously disdaining the loud, silly conversation and quarrels of Ginny, Joanne, and Helen at the other table. Sometimes they had to accept the company of one of the three who had quarreled recently with the other two. Tonight Lucy saw that Carol was hurrying ahead to sit with the others, still nursing the grudge of the door-answering episode. Well, if Carol wanted to be that dumb, it was all right with her—she'd sit by herself.

"Smells like spaghetti." Ginny's announcement was followed, as usual, by her meaningless giggle. Lucy knew immediately that Ginny meant it as a bid for company at the second table. She was a little sorry to be robbed of her isolation, but half a friend was probably better than none at all. She ought to be sitting with someone when Helen started sounding off to Sister Marian. Helen, Joanne, and Carol had already rattled through grace and were ladling sauce onto plates of spaghetti. They whispered archly and made elaborate pretense of stifling their laughter when Lucy and Ginny walked in together.

The second table held an enormous bowl of pale spaghetti beside a nearly empty bowl of sauce. Lucy studiously put butter, salt, and pepper on her spaghetti.

"Hey, you took our sauce." Ginny leapt to the bait, then remembered to giggle. "Come on, bring that sauce over here."

They continued eating in a dumb show of enormous appetite.

"I'll just sit here until Sister comes up. I'll show her what you did. No kidding, you're eating all our sauce." Ginny spoke with the edge of anxiety that always lay beneath the surface of the giggle. She pushed back her chair and marched over to the other table. Lucy noticed that the waistband of her skirt was rolled over and wrinkled by the strip of fat hung loosely around her middle.

"We're helping you diet, dahling," said Joanne throatily as she emptied the sauce bowl.

Ginny flounced back to her place and heaped a huge pile of spaghetti on her plate. She poked at the mound with her fork a few times and moved it around experimentally.

"Looks like worms to me," she said gloomily. Then she giggled.

"Excuse me, please. Somehow I've lost my appetite," Lucy said sarcastically and left the table. She almost bumped into Sister Marian in the doorway of the dining room.

"Good evening, Lucy. Did you have a nice visit?"

"Yes, Sister."

"How was Mother?"

"Fine, Sister."

"Aren't you eating dinner tonight?"

"I'm not hungry."

She tried to work her way past Sister Marian. She didn't want to be there when Helen started to complain.

"Sister, they took all our sauce," Ginny squealed.

"Girls, you didn't do that, did you?" No one could ask questions as helplessly as Sister Marian. It made you wonder why she was ever assigned to a place like St. Michael's.

"Yes, they did, Sister. Lucy started eating hers without any sauce. It was Helen's idea, I know she just wanted to get even because . . ."

"Shut up, you big baby," Helen said fiercely, and Lucy noticed that she had her left cheek covered with her hand.

"Well, I don't know what you're mad about," Ginny whined. "I didn't blame you, really, after Lucy . . ."

"Shut up, I said," Helen repeated, and Ginny slumped back into her chair.

Sister Marian's eyes filled with an expression of sorrow that made them look large and luminous as she turned from one girl to another. "Is anyone going to tell me what's the matter?" she asked, too gently. The question hung on the air like unripe fruit. "And I was coming up to give you a piece of good news," she murmured sadly.

"Oh, tell us, Sister," Ginny said, and she giggled, recovering instantly from her attack of injured feelings. The other four looked at her contemptuously to conceal their own interest.

"You'll have to wait five minutes, I have an errand to run," Sister said, and moved swiftly out of the dining room.

Lucy went on into the dormitory. Back in the dining room she could hear them all guessing what Sister's news might be—new clothes, something new for the lounge . . . maybe the stereo they'd been asking for. Ginny, predictably, was imagining pizza pies and steak dinners. Lucy opened her locker and reached into the coat pocket for the pieces of broken Delft. She arranged them on the bedspread and knelt down beside the bed, trying to discover some pattern in the shattered fragments. It was probably hopeless, but her fingers moved stubbornly, fitting one piece against each of the others until she found the matching sides of a blue flower. But there were so many pieces, and some had no markings at all on them. She closed her eyes wearily and rested her head on the bed.

"What's this, Lucy?"

She hadn't heard Sister Marian's footsteps. These nuns with their rubber-heeled shoes were worse than a bad conscience.

"It's some old thing my mother was throwing away. I thought Marcella might like it if I could fix it," Lucy said.

"It's lovely." Sister spoke genuinely and began sorting through the pieces, trying one against the other. "Was it a vase?"

"It was a shoe—it *is* a shoe," Lucy said.

"Are you sure you have all the pieces?" Sister asked.

"I think so. I had it in my coat pocket, you can check," Lucy said. Her fingers went back to the puzzling-out of the fragments.

"And is this some old thing your mother was throwing away, too?" Sister Marian held out the pack of cigarettes reproachfully. "Lucy, you know what Sister Christine said about smoking. You'll have to stay upstairs next Saturday night."

"I don't care, Sister, I just don't care. Sister Christine might think it's some big deal to go downstairs and watch television with dozens of idiots in bathrobes and hair rollers, but it's not my idea of a big time. I'd rather be up here by myself anyway." She worked in silence on the shoe for a full minute, with Sister Marian standing beside her. Finally she looked up and said, "Were you planning to stand there and watch me all evening?"

"No, dear. I was waiting for you to put that away and come to the dining room. I went down to the kitchen and brought up a bowl of sauce for you and Ginny."

"But, Sister . . ." Lucy was going to say that she didn't want to eat anything, but Sister Marian, standing there holding the cigarettes so awkwardly, looking far sorrier than Lucy felt, was more than she could deal with. Sister was so kind she usually robbed you of the satisfaction of being mean.

"Okay, Sister. I'll put this away for now. Are you planning to smoke the rest of those?"

"I'll give them to Mr. McClure. He likes to smoke down in the furnace room." She thrust them into her pocket, the pocket that could on a moment's notice produce needle and thread, a piece of candy, a fancy Band-Aid. Sister Marian was great for the small crisis, the quick sympathy. If any nun at St. Michael's could be called popular, it would be Sister Marian, with her young face blooming like an unexpected flower from under the half moon of white that held the short, black scrap of a veil. It was a delicate, fine face, easily wilted by disappointment when one of "her girls" failed to measure up in some way. Sister

Marian never got angry about anything; she just drooped sadly, not seeming to understand that some people would just as soon step on a wildflower as over one, or that some people might even find a certain satisfaction—a relief, almost—in doing just that. Lucy put the last pieces of Delft back in her coat pocket and followed Sister into the dining room.

The girls were still there: Carol, Helen, and Joanne at one table, by now growing giddy at one another's exaggerations as to what Sister's "news" might be, and Ginny alone at the other table, happily tucking into a well-sauced plate of spaghetti. Lucy ignored a sudden sense of loathing for Ginny and sat down across from her, taking only a token portion of spaghetti and sauce. Sister Marian pulled up a chair at their table and sat down.

I've just been talking to Sister Christine, and I have some news for you about next Saturday night."

"I thought you said you had a piece of *good* news," Lucy said loudly. Sister's face wilted and the others snickered. Lucy savored her small triumph while Sister studied the backs of her hands for a moment. Then she went on.

"You'll all have to put on a nice skirt and sweater and get your hair out of rollers for Saturday night."

"Oh, Sister!" The wail came in chorus.

"That's one way to cut down on our television watching," Carol said flippantly. "Well, I guess I'll just stay upstairs."

"I'll keep you company," Lucy said, edging her way back into grace. She enjoyed the private pleasure of accepting her own punishment so painlessly.

"Why *do* we have to get dressed on Saturday, Sister?" Ginny asked the obvious question with her mouth full, as though it weren't important enough to interrupt her eating. The others all viewed her with explicit disgust and Lucy moved her chair slightly over toward the other table. Sister Marian glanced gratefully at Ginny.

"On Saturday night all the other girls in the house will stay in their own dormitories or lounges; the television lounge downstairs will be strictly for you"—Sister paused, then added—"*and* your guests of the evening." The girls clustered around the nun with a scraping of chair legs against the wooden floor. Lucy was back in the circle, and even Ginny seemed to find the conversation more appetizing than the spaghetti.

"Sister Christine and I thought you girls might enjoy records and dancing with some nice boys . . ."

"Oh, Sister! Really?"

"I know just what I'm going to wear."

"Joanne, you're the only one they'll want to dance with."

"Lucy, can I wear your red skirt?"

"But, Sister, we don't *know* any nice boys."

The last observation put a sudden stop to the flurry of remarks and they all looked expectantly at Sister Marian, who was enjoying the sensation she had created.

"Well, you should know quite a few of them after Saturday night. Sister Christine wrote to Brother Xavier at St. Francis High and asked him to invite ten or so juniors and seniors."

"Ten or so! We can each have two!"

Everyone laughed, then immediately began speculating on clothes, dancing, boys.

"Did the Brother say they'd come?" someone asked.

"He was sure there'd be at least ten or a dozen," Sister said.

"Can we have dates with them after this? I mean, *if* they want us to?"

"I wonder how tall they'll be."

"Is Sister going to let them smoke? Really, Sister, you know most seniors *do* smoke."

By now all five girls were huddled around the chair where Sister Marian sat like a magician at a children's entertainment. Joanne was already unconsciously twisting curls at the nape of her neck; Ginny was stuffing her blouse into her skirt. Lucy and Carol sat in identical poses, bodies shifted slightly forward, feet wrapped around the finials of the chairs, hands clasped tightly on their laps, like children who have been promised a prize for good behavior.

"You just leave the details to Sister Christine. She'll plan a good party, you can be sure of that." Sister Marian's eyes were moist with excitement, and she smiled fondly at her strange family. "Right now you should all load these dishes onto the cart and get them downstairs before they finish and lock up in the dishroom. We have a whole week to work on hairdos, wardrobes, and other crucial problems." She stood up then, and it was as though a formal meeting had been dismissed. The girls scattered off and soon there were sounds of tubs being filled, locker doors being opened, bureau drawers slammed shut in the ritual rush to get downstairs to watch Friday night television.

Lucy began piling the plates, glasses, and silver onto the cart. Sister Marian started to call the others back to help, but Lucy stopped her. "Sister, could I skip television tonight instead of next Saturday?" She asked the question as casually as if she were requesting tea instead of coffee at a restaurant.

"Of course." Sister matched Lucy's perfunctory tone. Neither looked at the other.

"And, Sister, don't make them come back for the dish cart. I'll take it down myself. I want to stop off and see Marcella before she goes down to television, anyway."

Sister Marian stood for an instant looking at Lucy so intensely that it might have been a hard look, except for the softness and warmth in her eyes. Lucy glanced away, embarrassed and suddenly close to tears. She managed to mumble, "Thank you, Sister," and ducked her head out of reach as Sister went to rumple her hair. She couldn't bear to have anyone touch her just then. She half heard, half supplied the "God bless you, Lucy" that Sister Marian called softly after her.

On the way up from the dishroom, Lucy imagined the noises coming from every corner of the building as motors and engines running a huge machine. In the basement there was the sound of the dishwasher and the voices of the girls stacking the clean dishes. On the first floor, the sounds had a filtered quality. A typewriter ticked away in Sister Christine's office, muffled by the closed door; the rush of traffic in and out of the Sisters' Community Room was softened by the rubber-soled shoes that most of the nuns wore. Across from the Community Room, the light from behind the chapel door poured a spill of dull luster into the hall and cast grotesque shadows against the wall each time someone came out. Even the sound of twenty-some girls gathered in the huge lounge at the front of the house was unreal, softened by the thick carpeting and heavy draperies of a generous benefactor, the required modulation of sound on the television they had all come to watch, and the invisible but potent control of Sister Christine in her office across the hall. Lucy passed the closed door and permitted herself a private grimace of distaste for no particular reason. On the second floor she paused briefly at the landing to listen to the little ones chanting their night prayers in singsong fashion, warmly, sleepily, faithfully asking their guardian angels to "watch and guard, to rule and guide" them through the night. She hurried on to the third floor, where Marcella lived with the age group that was allowed to call itself "pre-teen," a term that delighted the nine-to-twelve-year-olds and was ridiculed and resented by Lucy's own company on the fourth floor, all of whom were at least fifteen. Lucy stuck her head in the doorway and saw, with relief, that Marcella had not gone downstairs yet. Everyone else had vanished from the dormitory.

In the light of the bedside lamp at the far end of the room Marcella crouched, one knee on the floor, the other nearly touching her chin, staring at the doll village under construction. Her right arm was curved, at rest, along the updrawn knee, while the left was outstretched in the air, utterly still. Marcella's fingers held a single Popsicle stick like a wand.

"Marcella?" Lucy waited, and when the figure remained frozen in tableau, she called again, more insistently, "Marcella!"

The left hand opened, dropped the stick, and joined the right hand, forming a clasped circle around the knee. There was no other indication that she had heard Lucy.

"Marcella, for pete's sake, will you come off it!" Lucy spoke with irritation and snapped on the main light switch. As light stung every corner of the huge room, her eyes, accustomed to the dimness of corridors and stairways, blinked owlishly. Marcella jumped up, danced around to face Lucy, and smiled. Her smile was luminous. It always was. Marcella's smile had nothing to do with what was going on around her. If it seemed terribly appropriate at times, more often it was a maddening communication of some inner secret, some delight that no one could fathom. Marcella was as apt to smile that way in the middle of a reprimand as when receiving a reward. Standing there in a long white flannel nightgown, her long black hair hanging thickly about her shoulders, the incongruously fair skin glowing with high color, the blue-dark eyes smiling too, Marcella made Lucy think of a dark angel, or a beautiful witch.

"Hi, Marcella. Aren't you going down to watch television?"

"Nope. There's more interesting things going on up here."

"Such as . . . ?"

"Oh, somebody's mother left me a box with a hundred more sticks, and I'm thinking how to use them. I wish it was summer," she said with sudden passion. "I'd have all I needed then. This building business is rough in wintertime." She spoke as seriously as the general contractor of a building project, and Lucy didn't know whether to smile or tell her not to take it so seriously.

"Besides, I'm thinking of more poems," she said suddenly, and smiled again.

"More poems?" Lucy asked.

"Yes, I wrote one today. Would you like to read it? How was Mother?"

Lucy took the questions in deliberate succession. "I'd

love to read your poem, and Mother was fine. She wanted to know how you were. I told her about your village, and next time I'll tell her about your poems. Sister would probably let you send this one to her if you'd like."

"Would I like, would I love, would I not like, would I not love . . ." Marcella chanted the phrases as though they were an exercise in grammar. "Yes, I would like," she finally affirmed, and rummaged in the drawer of her small desk among pencil stubs, erasers, paper clips, and bits of string, emerging with a piece of ruled paper torn from a copybook. Lucy took it and sat down on the edge of the bed to read.

Oh, once there was a honey bee.
Its wings were fine and fair to see,
Its velvet body striped with sun,
It met the flowers one by one.

One summer day when he flew up
To drink out of the flower cup
He found each one was closed up tight
And he went hungry all that night.

The next day and the next he flew
To find his food of honey dew
But not a single bud would give
The sweetness that would make him live.

And so he stung each one to death,
He stung till he was out of breath.
Without his food he quickly died,
And no one cared, and no one cried.

"Oh, Marcella," Lucy said angrily, "why do you have to do weird things *all* the time? I mean, building a nice village is okay, but *you* have to turn it into some full-time religious project, and now this poem—you start a nice poem, and turn it into some crazy, ugly spook story. I swear, you're as bad as Mamma."

"I'm glad it reminded you of Mamma." Marcella's blue eyes kindled with dark excitement. "I wrote it for her, you know. Don't you think she'll like it?"

"She probably will," Lucy said tiredly.

"I'm writing one for you next, and then one for Sister Christine. Maybe I'll write a book of poems for the whole world. How long do you think that would take, Lucy?" Marcella had gotten up off the floor and joined Lucy on the edge of the bed, where she sat smoothing her nightgown over her updrawn knees. "Poems are better than Popsicle sticks, I guess. You don't have to wait for people to bring things so you can do something." She sat quietly for a moment, then got up and went to her elaborate village and began methodically breaking up the tiny buildings that had been painstakingly glued together.

"Marcella, are you crazy or something?" Lucy spoke sharply, but Marcella went on with calm efficiency.

"Of course I am," she answered softly. Then, as if with a rush of wings, she jumped up from her demolished village and ran back to the bed where her sister sat, smiled with lightning quickness, and laughed down at Lucy.

"Lucy, you're always serious. You're even serious about being happy. I know what you mean, but you're wrong. You just don't understand." Marcella had stopped laughing, but the smile endured as though a current of delight had been turned on somewhere inside her.

"Come downstairs and watch television with me," she invited, still smiling.

Lucy shook her head. "I can't. Lost my Friday privilege." She managed to smile back at her sister, but her smile was only an echo of Marcella's. "But you'd better get downstairs, because next Saturday you're going to be up, and I'm going to be down." She had freighted the statement with all the overtones of confidential, inside information, but Marcella only cocked her head in momentary puzzlement, then pulled on slippers and robe and darted away, crossing the dormitory in an improvised dance among the beds, chairs, and desks. At the doorway she turned, threw a kiss, and sang out, "Bye-bye, Lucy Lucifer." She disappeared into the gloomy cave of the hallway, her sudden, wonderful laughter echoing over her shoulder all the way downstairs. Lucy blinked her eyes as though dazed by sudden sun. Then she switched off the dormitory light and went upstairs, where the problems and puzzles took the simpler form of a shattered Delft shoe.

## Chapter 3

Lucy lolled back in the too-hot tub, her feet propped on the faucets, studying her toenails. They were smooth and pink, rimmed by a neat white edge. She glanced automatically at her fingernails, observed how they were chewed down to the quick, wished briefly that they looked as nice as her toenails, and pulled the plug. She had gotten the last turn at the tub by volunteering to take Carol's place in the dishroom. This way you didn't have the other four banging on the door, breathing down your neck before you even had a chance to enjoy the luxury of privacy.

But tonight there wasn't really time to loiter. Joanne had promised to do Lucy's hair; Carol had lent her her precious blue cashmere sweater because it went so perfectly with the plaid skirt she was wearing. Helen, who hadn't spoken to Lucy for days, had begun talking at dinnertime about different types of boys and what you should talk about to the different kinds.

"If there's a brainy type, you take him, Lucy," she said, and they all laughed inordinately. Lucy laughed with them. It was probably going to be a good party. Except for Ginny. There was nothing you could do about Ginny. She was a baby, a fat baby. Lucy hurried into her clean underwear, giving a final tug to the slip that clung damply to her small hips, and opened the door. The cooler air of the dormitory fanned in on her cheeks, which had turned rosy from the steam.

Joanne brushed hard; from the scalp to the ends of the hair her strokes were relentless, but you knew it was going to look good when she finished. Lucy relaxed under the mesmeric rhythm of it.

"That feels good, Jo."

"Looks good," Joanne replied with authority, lifting the hair from the nape of Lucy's neck. "You're one of the few heads of hair I know that doesn't need spray." Lucy was pleased by the remark. She closed her eyes. "Your mother teach you how to do hair?" she asked.

"Are you kidding?" Lucy could feel, rather than see, Joanne's eyes narrowing. "No, I've just got the knack, that's all. It's a God-given talent." An edge of mimicry crept into the last remark, but Lucy couldn't decide whom Joanne was mocking. She didn't really care. Joanne was doing important things with her hair, lifting it with her fingers, coaxing it into a fullness around Lucy's face.

"I could sit here forever like this," Lucy said.

"Well, sit all you like, but I'm going downstairs to see if these boys are for real. It's probably some huge practical joke of Sister Christine's." Joanne gave a final twist to the curl at the back of Lucy's head and put down the hairbrush. "You'll probably mess it up putting on your clothes," she said matter-of-factly, precluding any possibility of being thanked.

Lucy went over to her bed, where the clothes were laid out. She remembered Joanne's remark about messing up her hair, and stepped into the pleated skirt, then carefully shrugged into the borrowed blue sweater, stretching the neck wide with her fingers as she slipped it over her head.

"Hey, take it easy with the merchandise," Carol called out. "That item happened to cost thirty dollars, in case you didn't know."

"Okay, okay, do you want me to put your name and a price tag on it before I go down?" Lucy said.

"Oh, Carol, it's beautiful." The words, spontaneous and unplanned, sprang out of her with the soft, sudden feel of cashmere across her shoulders and arms. "I don't even look like myself," she said. "I don't even *feel* like myself."

Carol was turning from side to side to examine her appearance from every angle. Lucy wanted to tell her that the black jersey blouse was too tight, too low, that she was wearing too much eye makeup, that Sister Christine would have her down in the office first thing next morning for a lecture on modesty, style, taste, and all that went with it. She actually felt a little embarrassed about Carol's appearance.

"How do I look?" Carol asked.

"Sexy," Lucy answered, loading her voice with approval she didn't feel.

"How does it feel to be disguised as a woman?" Helen said. "We can introduce you as our housemother." Carol's eyes darted uncertainly from Helen to the mirror to Lucy. Lucy quirked the corner of her mouth to indicate silent contempt for Helen's remark. Reassured, Carol turned back for a final self-approving glance in the mirror.

Helen had been working a tube of pale pink lipstick over her mouth as she spoke, and the words came out in a flat, dull monotone. Everything about Helen came out that way; Lucy almost felt sorry for her, but you couldn't feel too sorry for someone you didn't like, and it was impossible for her to like Helen. Helen was sneaky—dull and sneaky. She lied about unimportant things, like telling Sister Marian she had done her laundry over the weekend and then wearing dirty underwear all the next week. She would take her bicycle out on a Saturday afternoon, come back at five o'clock, and tell them she had ridden out to the country, when other girls had seen her all afternoon in City Park lying on her back staring up at the sky. Once she had come home from a visit with her mother carrying a lavishly illustrated book about rare birds which she said was a gift from her uncle. Lucy, browsing through a downtown department store the following weekend, had seen a huge display featuring the book. That night she walked past Helen's desk, where the unopened volume lay, and casually muttered the single word, "Thief." Helen had gone pale for an instant, then replied, "I've got a thing or two on you, Brannan, that you wouldn't exactly like published." It was true. They all ferreted out the secrets, the wounds, and the shames of one another and used them when the frailer guise of friendship failed. No one was exempt; no one was immune.

"If we don't get downstairs, Joanne's going to have all the boys," Ginny giggled.

"When you get down there, they'll probably all grab their coats and run," Helen answered impassively. She replaced the cap on the lipstick, brushed a fine powder of dandruff from her dark sweater, and stood up to go. Ginny's round face puckered up as though she were going to cry. Lucy felt a stab of compassion, but when Ginny edged over to her and began stroking the sleeve of the sweater she was wearing, she jerked her arm away abruptly. "Keep your grubby paws off of me," she said savagely, and turned to Carol and Helen, deliberately excluding Ginny from her glance. The three started downstairs, with Ginny padding softly, anxiously, behind them.

Joanne was standing in the front hall with Sister Marian and Sister Christine. She marked the arrival of the other four with a giant inclusive wave of her arm. "Hurry up! It looks like a great party—not a single boy has showed up. Helen, can I have the first dance?" They all broke into nervous laughter, nudging one another and giggling helplessly. Even Sister Marian, her cheeks bright red with excitement, couldn't conceal the anxious smile that struggled in the corners of her mouth.

"I should think you'd be happy for the opportunity of composing yourselves," Sister Christine said coolly. She stood there, regally tall, slender, unyieldingly aristocratic in her bearing. Her composure, one of the invariables of existence, was among the few solid comforts the girls knew. Sister Christine was always going to be cool and poised and utterly direct with them. She was immediate with both praise and blame, easy to please but impossible to satisfy. The other nuns, if you studied them long enough, all offered some access to their inner selves. The girls knew some details of their pre-conventual existences, but Sister Christine remained impenetrable. Some said she had been a Philadelphia debutante, some said a New York chorus girl. Once Lucy had been certain it was the young face of Sister Christine who stared at her out of a photograph of the old St. Michael's girls hanging in the Bishop's Parlor. But when she checked the dates, she found that Sister Christine would have to be seventy years old to have been in that photograph. Curiously, Lucy had been disappointed by the obvious impossibility of it.

"While I'm thinking of it, let me remind you to give a special thank you to Sister Gratia tomorrow," Sister Christine began.

"Sister Gratia?" Ginny's high-pitched squeal traveled along everyone's nerves.

"Yes, Sister Gratia, and do *modulate,* Ginny. Sister thought that your guests, being young and male, might be as interested in food as they are in you. She didn't leave the kitchen all day. If you get tired of dancing, or if you can't think of anything to talk about, take the boys over to the Bishop's Parlor."

Sister Christine moved soundlessly to the massive entrance, followed by the five girls, who clumped together protectively. She turned to the right and snapped on the light switch. The heavy crystal chandelier flooded the usually gloomy room with light. Against the east wall, two mahogany library tables, pushed together, held polished silver platters heaped with cold chicken, sliced ham, roast beef. There were bowls of mustard, pickles, relishes, nuts. There were baskets of rye bread and crusty white rolls, platters of deviled eggs. Two high layer cakes with chocolate frosting flanked a huge cut-glass bowl brimming with pale golden punch.

"Oh, Sister!" the five chorused approval.

"I'm glad you're pleased with it. Now let me have a look at all of you. Ginny, your hair is quite nice this evening; when you shed a few pounds, you're going to surprise everyone. Joanne, I hope you didn't think this was a *masked* ball; I'm afraid you've outdone yourself with the eye makeup."

"Helen, dear, straighten your shoulders. If you hold your rib cage high, every posture problem automatically corrects itself." The five girls all breathed deeply and stood taller with unconscious unanimity. "Lucy, I don't believe I've ever seen you looking more put together; quite nice, really. Carol, how on earth did you arrive at that costume? I'll certainly have to begin some sort of wardrobe check if you start decking yourself out in that fashion. I could lend you my thick black shawl as a cover-up, but I think it will be simpler for you to run upstairs and change into something more suitable."

Carol's eyes darkened with resentment. "I might have known you wouldn't like it," she shot back.

"No, I certainly don't, and I don't think anyone else does either."

"If you recall, I made a remark in that direction," Helen began airily.

"Look, you skinny, flat-chested, jealous . . ."

"Carol, go change your clothes," Sister Christine cut into the angry exchange with surgical efficiency. At the same moment the front doorbell pealed through the halls. Sister Christine put her hands on Carol's shoulders and turned her in the direction of the staircase. Then she went quietly to open the front door.

Lucy felt a moment of something like loyalty to Carol. "We all ought to go upstairs until Carol gets changed," she said. "Sister Christine always pulls this sort of stunt—we ought to just let *her* talk to these boys until we're good and ready to come down—sometimes I think she enjoys *humiliating* us . . ." Her voice trailed into silence as she realized no one was listening to her. They were all edging cautiously, uncertainly toward the knot of boys Sister Christine had greeted at the door and was divesting of coats and gloves. There were sounds of throat clearing, foot shuffling, and general discomfort as Sister Christine drew the two groups together. "Joanne, Helen, Ginny, Lucy," she singled out each of the girls with a gracious hand, "may I introduce Jim Norris, Tom Naulty, Owen O'Brien, George Shelly, Peter Frazier, and Tony Ruggerio." In the embarrassed moment of exchanging hellos, no one marveled at Sister Christine's ability to match six new names and six new faces with immediate accuracy.

"I'm sure that with your combined energies we can get a rug rolled back for dancing." Sister Christine moved to the large television lounge as she spoke, rescuing the moment from awkwardness by giving the boys something to do with their hands and feet. They set to work with relief, and Lucy studied each of them briefly.

Two of them, Jim and Tom, she thought, were too short. The next two would do; she saw that they were tall enough, not exactly good-looking, but they would do. One of them had red hair and an overly red face, but he seemed least embarrassed about being here. The other was dark-haired, wore glasses, and had very large ears. Of the remaining two, one made Lucy nervous just looking at him. His face, his ears, his neck were covered thickly with angry purplish-red pimples. His eyes, which were dark and expressive, begged forgiveness for the condition of his skin. From time to time, when his hands found themselves idle, one or the other of them would dart up to his cheek and unconsciously finger a blemish. Lucy was terrified that he might ask her to dance. She looked at the last of the boys and found herself involved in a mutual inspection. Whoever he was, he had obviously singled her out already and he was marvelous to look at. He was tall and moved with easy assurance. His jacket was tweedy and expensive. His eyes were unbelievably blue and direct and when he caught her glance he smiled and winked. "Oh God, please let him like me," she thought, and smiled back. He ducked his head down in something that was half nod, half promise, and walked over to the nuns.

"I think we've gotten the rug safely out of the way. Is there anything else that needs moving, Sister?" he asked.

"Only us, and we can take care of ourselves," Sister Christine answered coolly, but the girls all knew she was pleased. "I'll be right across the hall in my office, and Sister Marian is going to help me with some paperwork. If you need us, just knock." Everyone murmured something, none of it important enough to emerge clearly, and then the nuns were gone and they were alone with the boys from St. Francis.

"Hey, any of you know how to dance? None of us do." That was the boy with the red hair, and they all laughed for a moment, then dropped into abrupt silence.

"Okay, Pete, you can find out which one of these girls wants to go over football plays with you; Lucy and I are going to get some music going."

She was seized by a sudden sense of panic. She hadn't caught his name; she didn't know how to talk to a boy like this. She followed him over to the record player and lifted an armload of records from the rack, handing them to him one at a time. He chose from the ones she handed to him, setting some aside with an air of imperturbable authority that made Lucy despise the rejects without even knowing which they were. When the music began, Lucy could hear, as though it were a faraway sound, the rushes and ebbs of beginning conversation among the others.

"But Joanne can imitate anybody's voice, or face. It's fantastic. Show Tony, Joanne," Helen was saying. "I'm afraid I haven't mastered *ears* yet," Joanne answered in her theatrically deep voice. There was an explosion of laughter, and Lucy looked just in time to see the boy with the large ears cock his head forward and wiggle both ears. Helen, encouraged by her initial success, began demonstrating a new dance step to Jim and Tom, the two short ones, who had apparently been attracted to her smallness. Ginny, her face bathed in an excess of pleasure, was squealing idiotic appreciative remarks to Pete, the redhead, who actually *had* begun explaining football plays to her. From time to time she bobbed, like an inflated water boy, toward the boy with the bad skin to cry, "Oh, he didn't *really* say that to the coach, did he?" "Tell her, George," Pete would insist. Then, assured that it was true, Ginny would pucker up her lips, roll her eyes, and say, "Ooooh." Lucy cringed inwardly at the sound of it, but somehow, incredibly, they all seemed to be enjoying themselves.

"Pete'll have her out on the practice field tomorrow," Lucy's partner said with faint distaste in his voice, and she answered, acidly, "Ginny is really a first-string dope." He encouraged her banal remark with a smile, and they began dancing. He was an excellent dancer. Lucy felt detached from herself, just a single facet of the light, motion, and color that had possessed the room as she followed him, matching her step, her movements to his. At one point, his hand touched her shoulder, then moved down the length of her arm to the wrist with firm deliberation. "Nice," he remarked. Lucy was startled. Then, realizing with relief that he spoke of the sweater and not of her, she shook her head insistently and said, "It's not mine."

"Oh?" His single syllable invited her to explain, but she didn't want to talk about Carol, who was still upstairs, alone, furious, and humiliated, and she bit her lip in vexation, not knowing what to say. The music had stopped momentarily between records and he stood there looking at her quizzically, waiting for her to say something. Her tongue was numb. She could hear the confused blur of sound in the background; as though they were in a picture hanging on the wall, she could see the rest of the group enjoying themselves, relaxed now in conversation with one another, trading partners for dances. Pete had worked his way out of the football diagrams and showed himself surprisingly graceful in the dance he was doing with Joanne. Ginny, her small plump hands clasped together earnestly, was explaining the division into age groups of the girls at St. Michael's, as George listened with obvious interest. Somewhere along the conversation route, the two of them seemed to have forgotten her fat, his blemishes. Helen had a dreamy translucent look of joy on her face and Lucy noticed that Jim was holding her hand. Lucy despised them all in their easy satisfaction. Tom, momentarily unattached, walked over to Lucy.

"I see that Owen O'Brien's got the luck of the Irish going for him again. They all say you're the smartest, the best-looking . . ." Tom jerked his thumb back in the direction of the other girls and looked at Lucy as though he expected her to confirm his high opinion of herself. She felt chained in discomfort. Why did he have to begin a conversation so ridiculously? It was impossible to reply to a remark like that. She smiled sourly.

"Well, she's certainly not the greatest conversationalist," Owen said with finality. "Maybe you can pry a remark or two out of her. Let me know if you have any luck. I'm cutting out of here." He slid his hands into the pockets of his trousers and ambled out of the room. Lucy hated him.

"That's an awfully nice friend you've got there," she said viciously.

"Ah, don't take Owen seriously. He's always like that. You know, good looks, lots of money, lots of problems. We all sort of put up with plenty from him. His parents are divorced, you know, and that's rough. You don't know what it does to a guy to spend half his life with his father and the other half with his mother . . ." A sudden embarrassed horror paralyzed Tom's face as he realized what he was saying. He stood there grinning idiotically, his words frozen in his throat.

At that moment Lucy knew with apocalyptic certainty that the normal world was absolutely and permanently inaccessible to her. It would never be any different from this, she realized, and the realization made her feel both frantic and giddily free. She impaled Tom with a furious glance that was all out of context with the soft sweet voice she assumed for her next remark. "That's really rough, you're right." She shook her head sympathetically. "It makes you realize how lucky the rest of us are." She swung her head to clear away the tears that had begun to swim dangerously in her eyes. "Why, every night I just kneel down and thank God my mother is only an alcoholic. Every morning when I brush my teeth I say, 'Sweet Jesus, watch over my father, wherever he may be,' and then, after I spit the mouthful of rinse water down the drain, I say 'Amen.' "

"I'm sorry, Lucy, golly, I didn't . . ."

"No, you didn't, did you," she cut him short, allowing her voice to grow loud and reckless, and then she let him watch the tears streak down her face for just a second before she rushed out of the room and blindly climbed the stairs to join Carol in the dormitory.

# Chapter 4

She hadn't been able to explain it to Sister Christine the morning after the party when she was called to the office to defend her extraordinary behavior.

"Don't you see, Sister, I just hate this Home. I hate every person, place, and thing about it. I'd run away from here tomorrow, but I have no place to run to, no one to run to, nothing—NOTHING." She tried to shout the last word, but it came out in a choked, furious stammer and she dropped her face into her hands to cry again.

"Lucy, lift your face up while I'm talking to you."

The quiet authority in Sister Christine's voice commanded obedience. Lucy straightened up and glared across the desk. "Oh, it's easy for you to sit there and preach away at me; you've got all the answers and all the questions there in that nasty file cabinet. It makes me sick to think of you going over everybody's dirty problems in those phony clean white folders. You and the social workers. It's fun, isn't it? Kind of like a giant jigsaw puzzle, trying to put us all together. Well, let me tell you something, Sister. You don't know what it's like to have every twitch of your soul that shows turned into a notation for your record. It's indecent, that's what it is. Hell won't be any different, and it won't be any worse. You'll find out I'm right when you get there. And I'll tell you one more thing about your puzzle game. The reason it doesn't work, the reason you can't get the picture to work out, is that half the pieces are missing. We're none of us real whole people here, Sister, we're nothing but parts and pieces with knobs sticking out that have nowhere to fit and spaces with nothing to fill them."

Lucy felt wonderfully cleansed and peaceful after her outburst. She had a sense of something precious, infinitely fragile but safe from harm, lodged in the center of her being. It had been a long time since she was last aware of that. No one could touch it, it was her own and it was a mystery, even to her. It was made of nothing, and everything. In a moment of awareness, like this one, it seemed impossible that it could ever be forgotten, unfelt. And still, most of the time, it was the splinter of glass, lodged in the heart, that Lucy was aware of. Perhaps that was the same thing out of its proper place.

"I'm sorry, Sister Christine, I didn't mean that. But I did," she added instantly, compelled by a sudden urgency for order and truth.

"I hope you did mean it, Lucy. You needn't ever apologize to me for the truth—seeing or saying it. And I like your notion of the puzzle. It's very good. That's exactly what I have to work with, in fact, but I don't think of it as a game; I would scarcely call it fun. None of us are whole, Lucy. That's what life is all about—making the space for the things that have nowhere to go, cutting them off if they shouldn't be there in the first place. And creating what's needed to fill the empty spaces. None of us can do it alone, Lucy, none of us. We all need one another. The person with every piece fitting properly is the rare one—the saint. But we can never stop trying, and we can't let ourselves be satisfied with something that doesn't really belong in the picture. It's not easy, but it's the only way."

Sister Christine looked at her with unsparing directness. Lucy knew it was her turn to say something, and that Sister Christine would wait with unnerving patience for her to say it.

"But it's easy for you, Sister. You're grown up—you're done."

"It's never easy, Lucy." She shook her head slowly, with insistence. "And it's never done."

"But at least you know how to begin—you have something to work with."

"Nothing more than you have, Lucy. Body and soul are all we have to give."

The words hung on the quiet of the room. A clock ticked. Outside, two birds chattered with glassy brilliance, then stopped abruptly. Somewhere a door slammed.

"I'll try, Sister. I'll try to grow up." She attempted a laugh, but it caught in the back of her throat like the edge of a sob. "I really don't have any choice, do I?" she asked raggedly.

49

And now three weeks had passed since the party. The early hopes of a busy dating life that the evening had engendered in Ginny, Joanne, and Helen had soured and shriveled into a hard core of disappointment and bitterness. For two days after the party, Lucy and Carol had eaten creamed chicken and cold beef suppers in disdainful silence at a separate table, while the other three turned each forkful of food into an occasion for reminiscence, exchanging information and futuristic planning.

"It's pretty bad when a stale deviled egg turns into a love token," Lucy remarked at one mealtime.

"No worse than a seventeen-year-old girl turning into a bawling jackass," Joanne replied airily. Lucy had no answer. The time since that evening had become a sort of season in its own right, a season whose climate was unfeeling detachment. She had told Carol everything she could remember about the party. The details of her own behavior were rendered as completely as her description of the boys. "You really didn't miss anything," she insisted.

The wounded look in Carol's eyes gradually healed over as the other three gave up talking about their adventures, past and projected. Only two things remained as indirect but constant reminders that something out of the ordinary had taken place. Ginny had begun dieting with a ferocity that astonished everyone. There were bruised-looking, bluish circles under her eyes, and an irritable tenseness to her mouth, but she was losing weight. And Helen, after her letter to Jim, obviously misaddressed, had been returned with "addressee unknown" stamped in purple across the envelope, had suddenly shifted from dull, subversive meanness to outbursts that frightened them all, even though they shrieked with laughter when she kicked a chair across the dining room, and whistled and cheered like men at a cockfight when she grabbed Joanne by the hair in the course of a trivial argument.

Lucy kept out of all their fights. She wanted nothing to disturb the tentative peace that lay just out of reach. She felt, superstitiously, that she was somehow being tested. She had no idea what for, but she understood the nature of the test. She had to avoid involvement, she could not engage in any major episode. If she succeeded, there would be a reward. She had no idea what the reward would be. But she knew it was something she needed desperately. There was only one thing wrong, one piece missing from the elaborate notion she had constructed. She had no idea how long the test would last. Perhaps for one more day, perhaps for a year, but she was sure she would know when it was over. There would be a sign. There would have to be a sign. She was trying to explain it to Carol.

The two of them were working on the Delft shoe at Lucy's desk one Saturday afternoon. All the others had disappeared in the elasticity of the weekend routine. The toe had been completely reconstructed and the small heel was beginning to take shape.

"Maybe when the shoe is finished," Carol said, understanding, but immediately wanting to complete Lucy's talismanic equation. "You know, when I was little, my father told me one time that God had the sky hooked up by a huge, invisible belt. He told me that every day God let the belt out one notch and that, when the last notch was let out, the sky would collapse on us and that would be the end of the world."

"Sounds as if he'd been reading *Henny-Penny*," Lucy laughed. "You know, 'The sky is falling, the sky is falling, I must run to tell the king.' "

"Oh, but it wasn't funny, Lucy."

Carol's voice had shifted suddenly from the indolent conversational tone to one of taut fear. Lucy sensed that Carol was talking to herself. She felt like an eavesdropper.

"I was so terrified. For months I would wake up and be afraid to open my eyes and look at the sky. I remember that winter, whenever there was a specially gloomy day, my father would say, 'Well, looks like He let it down quite a bit today; must not be very much left in that big belt.' He would use that horrible, falling sky to frighten me, to make me do what he wanted."

Lucy put down the piece of china she was holding and looked at Carol. Carol's fingers gripped each other so fiercely that her knuckles showed white. Unconsciously, she had begun breathing heavily, nervously, and Lucy found herself staring at the rise and fall of the third button on Carol's gray cardigan.

"What did he want you to do, Carol?" she asked quietly, puzzled.

"If I told you, I'd die." Carol's voice broke and she pressed her fingers into her eyes and rocked back and forth on the hard seat of the desk chair, shaking her hidden face back and forth in a negative motion of disbelief and despair. "I was afraid to die then, Lucy, I was only a little girl, I was so afraid to die, and he was my father. I had to do what he told me, Lucy, I had to. And he used God, and a falling sky, and darkness to frighten me. Oh, Lucy, he was my father."

A tingling paralysis crept over Lucy. It began in her

foot, which had gone numb from being tucked under her too long, and crept all the way up to her shoulders, so that she shuddered involuntarily as with a sudden chill. She felt repelled by some terrible knowledge she sensed Carol was about to confide. She wanted none of it, yet at the same time there was something compelling in the dark mystery. An obscene curiosity took hold of her, filling her with the sudden sensations of heightened perception. The piece of broken china she had picked up, as though to defend herself, was palpably cool and smooth under her fingers, the resinous smell of glue stung at her nostrils so sharply she could imagine the taste of it along her tongue. The colors stood out sharply; she marveled, for a moment, that she had never before noticed the intensity of blue against white. The wood grain on the scarred desk top seemed to reply with sound when she laid the small fragment down.

She thought of Carol's father. She had seen a photograph of him that Carol kept in her desk drawer, taking it out from time to time to study it with brooding concentration. He was a handsome man. The picture had been taken near some body of water and Carol's father had been sitting on the edge of a dock, wind lifting the thick shock of dark hair from his forehead, a white sweatshirt, tied by the sleeves, hanging loosely over broad shoulders.

She had envied Carol, as the others had; for most of them, there was a mythic quality about fathers. Like the rest, Lucy could scarcely remember hers. There had once been a home, a real family, and there was a man that you called "Daddy" when you were very small. But the edges blurred when you tried to remember more. Lucy had learned long ago not to ask Mamma about him; instead, she had imagined, invented, daydreamed into existence a

*53*

father curiously lacking in detail. When Mamma was happy, beautiful, when she did something that made you know you loved her, then Lucy was angry with her invented father—everything wrong became his fault. But when Mamma made you ashamed of her, or of yourself for belonging to her, then Lucy would know that some day she'd find her father and tell him how she had always loved him and looked for him. And he would tell her why he had gone to work one February morning and never come back.

"I don't know your father, Carol. I've never met him," Lucy said quietly, probingly. "Does he still live at home with your mother?"

Carol turned eyes dumb with animal anguish on Lucy.

"My father is in jail."

"What for?"

"Because of me."

It was like opening a package; layer upon layer of frail tissue needed to be drawn off. Lucy was ready for the next revelation when the quiet of the deserted dormitory was shattered. A strident, unrecognizable voice shrieked indistinguishable words of rage, then choked off into sudden silence that magnified the next sounds—a syncopated series of muffled thumps and soft insistent cries of pain. Then there was only a hint of the sound of weeping.

"Jesus, Mary, and Joseph," cried Lucy. "One of the little kids must have fallen all the way downstairs." She and Carol ran, hearts pounding, across the dormitory to the top of the wide wooden staircase. A dozen nuns and girls were already there, on the first landing, crowding around the crumpled form of Sister Marian. Lucy sucked in her breath. The nun lay still, eyes closed, a curiously childish astonishment curving her lips, which did not move at all. The small veil that covered the crown of her head had slipped back and a mass of short, dark curls hung forward on her brow. Her stockinged legs sprawled limply, like a rag doll's, from under the black skirt, twisted now above her knees, to inform the curious of a white lace-trimmed slip.

Sister Christine was there, on her knees, feeling with expert fingers for a pulse; several of the younger children were clustered around Helen, one of them clinging unconsciously to the hem of Helen's skirt and wiping her nose on the rough wool cloth. All of them were crying softly with Helen, a frightening, infantile whimper. Directly behind that group, smaller than Helen, taller than the little ones, was Marcella.

Marcella's eyes were large and round with wonder, lending an expression of pleasure to her face. She caught Lucy's glance and sent a brilliant smile across the terrible silence. Lucy felt the thunder of her heart greeting Marcella's smile. She wanted to cover her sister's face from the rest of the group. Then she realized that her own lips were smiling. She had no control over them, one corner of her mouth was twitching horribly. She ducked her chin down to her right shoulder and tried to press her face back to a proper expression. It was while she stood like that, chin tucked against the rounded shoulder joint, that she saw Marcella's mouth moving and heard, as if from far away, "Who killed Cock Robin? 'I,' said the sparrow. 'With my bow and arrow, I killed Cock Robin.' "

The words dropped into the silence like a blasphemy. Sister Christine jerked up her head. She had gone white, and her eyes blazed with anger and anguish. "Go back to your dormitories, all of you, and God pity the one who makes a sound. You'll wait there until you hear from me. And if it's not until midnight, so much the better. Sometimes I wonder how the dear Lord can bear to look on the creatures He's made."

They all stood there, transfixed by the fury in Sister Christine's voice.

"Go! Do you hear me? Go!" She got rid of the words as though they were a poison in her throat, then turned back to Sister Marian with the grieved tenderness of a mother. The girls moved off in numb silence, reluctant to leave the fragile security of one another's presence, struck with wonder at the strange thrill of tragedy. Over and over Lucy repeated the words, "Not Marcella. Oh God, not Marcella."

Back upstairs, each one busied herself with false, subdued activity. Joanne sat at her desk with a lengthy shorthand transcription exercise in front of her, running the pencil in her hand through her hair with the unbroken rhythm of a mechanical toy. Ginny unaccountably emptied every item of her bureau drawers onto her bed and began a patient reorganization of the contents. Each time she approached the end of the task, she would tumble sweaters, blouses, slips, pajamas into a common heap and begin a fresh ordering. Carol weeded her way through a bulging box of letters, photographs, and souvenirs, tearing each discarded item into minuscule scraps before dropping it into the wastepaper basket beside her desk. Lucy pretended to work on the shoe, but she found it impossible to keep from glancing nervously at Helen, who had provided herself with a sewing basket and a heap of dirty lingerie. Helen was removing safety pins from the straps of slips and bras and making repairs with feverish intensity. Several times Lucy saw Helen jab the long needle into her finger. Helen scarcely noticed; she seemed unaware of the pattern of spotted blood that her fingers were tattooing on her work. Lucy found herself compelled to watch the needle. She had lapsed into a hypnotic stare when she felt something pluck at her elbow. She wheeled sharply around on her chair and found herself face to face with Marcella.

"Get downstairs!" she whispered fiercely.

"I want to tell you something. Please?"

"Marcella, get downstairs. You'll make terrible trouble . . ."

"Trouble, trouble, who knows what trouble is? Do you, Lucy?"

"*Marcella.*" Lucy tried to insist on something by her tone of voice, but she wasn't sure herself what it was. She closed her eyes to shut out the smile she was afraid she might see on Marcella's face.

"Lucy, oh, please, Lucy." Lucy opened her eyes. Marcella was not smiling. The high color had gone from her cheeks; her face looked wizened, old yet almost embryonic, but for the eyes which appeared larger than life and which glittered with tears.

"Lucy, why did Mamma put us here? This is no home. This is a bad dream, Lucy. This is a bad place to live. Oh, Lucy, can't we go away? Can't you take me away and we'll just live together somewhere? And we'll have a little house with no stairs, just all on one floor. No going up and coming down. We'll be all alone, Lucy. No pushing. No pushing on the stairs, Lucy."

Marcella had dropped to the floor and placed her head in Lucy's lap. Lucy felt herself stroking Marcella's thick dark hair, lifting the heavy weight of it from off the fine, small neck and wrapping the ends in curls around her finger. Without looking, she knew the others were all staring, listening, even though the two of them had been speaking in whispers.

"Shhh, shhh," she whispered comfortingly to Marcella's unlistening ears, trying not to think what Marcella's terrible, incoherent account might mean, continuing to fondle the heavy dark hair as though that gesture alone could heal all the harms of the world. The sound of an ambulance siren drew nearer, the thread of sound wrapping in on itself, time after time, until it became the heavy wail that wound its way up the long front drive and sobbed to a stop at the front door. The girls all dropped what they had been doing and clustered at the dormer windows. Marcella jumped away from Lucy, suddenly electrified. She walked to the middle of the dormitory floor and assumed a center-stage posture. Color flooded back into her cheeks.

"Helen," she called softly, "Helen, oh Helen, oh Helen of Hell."

The others all turned from the window, slowly, as though peeled away from the activity at the front door by Marcella's call. Only Helen kept her face studiously glued to the window, but even from behind, the girls could see her shoulders begin to tremble.

"Helen, come away. If you stay there, you'll be turned to stone. Don't watch, Helen. Don't look at what you've done. If you watch, the devil will come and carry you away."

Helen turned around, her face white with furious agony. "Lucy Brannan," she stammered, and her voice was dark and thick. "Get that crazy sister of yours out of here or I'll kill her."

Lucy felt her face drain of blood. She joined the circle that had formed instinctively, protectively, around Marcella. Before any of them could decide what to do, Marcella ducked between Lucy and Carol and ran to Helen, lifted Helen's chin in her hands, and stood on tiptoe, to kiss each of Helen's cheeks, softly, slowly, deliberately.

"Helen, I love you," she said, shaking her head negatively. Then, with a sudden look of amazement, Helen sat down on the bare wooden floor, drew up her knees to cushion her head, and wept, huge choking sobs that sounded almost like laughing.

"Don't cry, Helen, don't cry. It's not worth it, unless it's for love," Marcella said. She dropped to the floor on one knee, pulled Helen's hand away from her face for a moment and scrutinized her crumpled expression, then let her head drop back onto the updrawn knee. Then Marcella looked around at the rest of them; the strange, hazardous smile blazed away on her face.

"Helen's really crying," she said simply and with great joy.

# Chapter 5

For supper they drank canned soup from paper cups, ate
sandwiches from cardboard plates, and tasted nothing.
There were no quarrels, there was no conversation. There
were not even dishes to do. A sense of gathering doom
clung to the evening shadows. The small cubicle at
the end of the dormitory where Sister Marian slept was
empty. The usual slot of light from under the door was
missing. The grotesque shadows thrown against the dormitory ceiling when Sister Marian undressed by the light of
the small bedside lamp were not there to comfort them
this night as they undressed and got into pajamas and
robes in grievous silence. It was the first time they had
waited in such dread anticipation of the dark; the familiar

shapes of beds, chairs, desks, and dressers were strange and ominous. Lucy was sure this was what Adam and Eve had felt like after the fall, before the judgment. There were terrors in this first night alone.

Lucy knelt down beside her bed and tried to say her prayers. The only thing she could think of was "Thank you, God, for letting it be Helen and not Marcella." That was scarcely a prayer, she thought, feeling guilty and vulnerable, as though anyone could look through the glassy feeling in her head and see what she was thinking. Better to say some formalized prayer, something with the words already there, and try to make it mean something, she decided.

"O my God, I am heartily sorry for having offended Thee, and I detest all my sins, not because I dread the loss of Heaven or the pains of Hell, but because they have offended Thee, O my God, who art all good and deserving of all my love. I firmly resolve, by the help of Thy grace, to confess my sins, to do penance, and to amend my life. Amen."

Heaven and Hell. They were both very far away and not really to be believed in. But to offend someone who was all good, who loved you and was deserving of all your love—you could be very sorry about that if you let yourself think about it. But what was left, if you let yourself go all soft and sorry about someone who really, truly loved you? And didn't it always turn out that they didn't really love you all that much anyhow? And where was God, who loved you so much, when Daddy ran away and when Mamma got drunk and messy about everything? Where was God, who art all good and deserving of all my love, when Marcella took that beautiful thing, whatever it was, in her and worked it around so crazily that you knew, no matter what, that something terrible was going to come of it, sooner or later?

O my God, I am hardly sorry . . . O my God, I am heartily sorry . . . O my God, I love Marcella, who is deserving of all my love. Oh my God, I love birds hopping on rooftops, and I love gardens full of flowers, because they have not offended Thee, and I love mothers who sing songs to their children at night, and I would love fathers if I could believe in them, O God, my Father, who art all good and deserving of all my love if I could only believe, really believe in you.

"Maybe this is what it's like to be going crazy," Lucy thought giddily. But her head was aching, so suddenly, so terribly. Dear God, oh, I will believe in you; I'll believe in everything, world without end, amen, if you'll just let Sister Marian be all right. I'll do penance and amend my life, amen, O God, please let her be all right. Helen couldn't help it. You know that, God, Helen didn't mean it. I don't hate Helen, God, please forgive her. I'll forgive her, God, if you'll forgive her. Let's forgive her, let's forgive everyone. Let's begin all over, God. Please give us this day our daily bread, give us this day our daily fresh clean page. Let us start over again.

Sister Christine appeared, without sound, without announcement, at the far end of the dormitory, her white face seeming to glow in the shadows. She picked up a chair from the far end of the dormitory, walked slowly toward them, and set the chair down in the center of the floor. She sat down, folded herself onto the chair, seeming suddenly too weary to stand for one more minute. The heavy, goodsy sound of her skirt rustled against the unyielding wood of the seat. The flesh of her hands and face looked drawn and exhausted.

"Dear little children," she said. The words, so unexpected, stunned them. "We have not loved one another enough. And because we have not loved enough, something cruel and frightening has touched all of us today.

"Sister Marian will be all right," she added quickly, reassuringly, but some large dread still fingered their hearts, choking off the expected sounds of pleasure and relief. "Sister has a broken leg, she's in Mercy Hospital, she'll stay there for a few days of tests and observation."

The clinical report was only a diversionary tactic, they all sensed that.

"But I am afraid that you will not see Sister any more. She will not be coming back to St. Michael's." The total silence was more telling than the expected chorus of protests. Grief numbed each face to a shape that matched the others. Sister Christine breathed softly, audibly. "Everything we do has an effect, and what we fail to do has its effect as well. We have to live in the world we create, and if we do not provide ourselves with love, and patience—if we take for our tools anger and hate, resentment or fear—then we will have to inhabit a world that crushes us, deprives us of light, a world so full of pitfalls that any step is a false one. Dear children, we cannot survive in a world where love is a luxury."

Lucy felt tears stinging her eyes. She longed to be redeemed from all the forces that held her back from that time and place where she could believe and love and trust. She knew there was such a time and place. She knew that somehow, somewhere, for each person, there had to be such a place. There was a point of love where all beginnings met; from this point, if it could only be discovered, Joanne could be beautiful, Ginny slender; that point could dissolve Carol's nameless terrors, open Helen and fill her with joy. It could unriddle the tangled mystery of Marcella; it would heal Lucy's terrible longings. Life would not have to be easier. Even Lucy could realize it might well be harder with great love as a burden—but it would be explicit. You would know where you were going, and you would have a place to rest and refresh your heart when you were sick, or faint, or too weary to go on. You would have a home for the heart.

Lucy squinted against the tears that were gathering in her eyes, turning the single light from the overhead fixture into a hundred tiny asterisks. Tears did that, multiplying your vision and reducing it at the same time. There were entirely too many tears here, she decided determinedly; they came too easily, they meant too little. If you cried about something, it made you feel as if you had done something, it made you feel as if you cared. What was it Marcella had said? "Don't cry, Helen. It's not worth it. Unless it's for love." Lucy wondered if Marcella understood all the things she said.

She realized Sister Christine had been saying something she had missed. There had been a transition from the strangely tender tone of address. Sister Christine was cool, direct, unsparing again.

"Sister Justin will arrive sometime tomorrow. I want you all to make her as welcome as you can. And if you find her different from Sister Marian, I want you to remember that difference is of your own making. Sister Justin didn't ask to come here, nor did Sister Marian ask to be transferred." There was an absoluteness about the remark that threatened them all. It was as if Sister Christine were daring them to complain, inviting them to make odious comparisons between Sister Marian and the unknown Sister Justin, that she might have an opportunity to remind them of their responsibility. They were all made uncomfortable by it.

"And now I think everyone has had a long-enough day. I'll sleep up here tonight, and there will be no radios on. Good night. And God bless you. I hope some of you might have grown up a bit today."

Sister Christine dropped her remark deliberately, like a smooth pebble in a quiet pool, and walked toward the cubicle at the end of the dormitory. Lucy climbed into bed and fell asleep before the last light blinked off.

Everyone woke early the next morning. All about them there was the odd feeling of being in a strange house, of having slept in an unaccustomed bed. The girls avoided talking to one another, except for perfunctory remarks, as they dressed for Sunday Mass. "Has anybody got a hat I can borrow?" Lucy asked.

"You just got a new hat last Sunday. Sister gave you a brown and black one."

"Well, I can't find it. That thing looked like a rotten mushroom anyway."

"Here, Lucy, you can wear this one." Ginny stood on tiptoe to pull a hat off the top shelf of her locker.

Joanne said, "That's it, dear, stretch hard, tuck in your bottom, verrrry good for the waistline."

Ginny blushed but said nothing. She bit her lower lip

for a moment, as though deciding whether or not to giggle. Then she stretched hard for the hat and handed it to Lucy. "It's a pretty dopey hat, but it *is* a hat."

For some reason, the incident struck Lucy as significant. Ginny had done something unapologetically, almost with dignity. She took the hat. It was red straw with a single white daisy sticking straight up from the band. It was a babyish hat, a ludicrous ugly thing. Lucy thought it the sort of hat that should have an elastic band for under the chin.

"Thanks, Ginny." She clapped the hat on her head, refusing herself so much as a glance in the mirror.

"Oh, I *hope* Hattie Carnegie doesn't show up in chapel for Mass this morning. She'd just *die* of envy." No one bothered to laugh at Joanne, and she went on combing her hair with the imperturbable air of a person who talks for her own amusement rather than for anyone who might happen to be within earshot.

"Anybody know anything about this Sister Justin?"

"Never heard of her."

"Where do you think she's coming from?"

"I don't know—probably the motherhouse. That's where they keep all the ones who are too old or too sick or too creepy to be doing a regular job. One day is pretty short notice to get her assigned here. She must be a real gem."

"We ought to enjoy ourselves today; it's probably the last day for a long while that life's going to be livable. Do you think she'll get here this afternoon or this evening?"

"Who knows? Ask Sister Christine."

"You ask Sister Christine. I'd rather not let her think I'm looking forward to anything. The way she talked last night really made my blood run cold. You know, it was almost like she was *warning* us about something."

"I'm sure she was," Lucy said with finality. She sat down on the edge of her unmade bed, tracing an invisible circle on the floor with the toe of her shoe. She refused to be curious about Sister Justin. Curiosity meant expectation, and if you expected something, the chances were pretty good that you'd be disappointed. It was far better to keep loose, to sit back and watch things, to make it all into a kind of mental movie where you could laugh when it was funny, even feel sad if it struck you that way, try to figure out what was coming next and how it would all end. It was kind of nice when you were right, and if you were wrong, it hadn't cost you anything but the price of admission. Lucy smiled wryly to herself; the thought had struck her that for this crazy show you didn't even have to pay to get in. It only cost you something if you let yourself turn into one of the actors. "Thanks, but no, thanks," she thought to herself. "I'll just watch, if you don't mind."

She was sitting there, pleased, cheered almost by the notion she had worked out in her mind, when her heart gave a sudden lurch, contradicting all her new-found detachment. Sister Christine had come into the dormitory with an unfamiliar nun whom she introduced, inevitably, as Sister Justin.

Sister Justin was small and incredibly thin. She was an old nun. Her skin was dry and waxy-looking but scarcely wrinkled. There were thin blue veins showing across her forehead, around her eyes, along the sides of her cheeks. She wore rimless glasses that magnified icy-gray eyes. Her teeth were large, slightly yellow, and between remarks she used them to bite back her lower lip, which hung loosely, with the air of an injury, along her lower gums. Her voice was thin, fine, and steely. As Sister Christine introduced her, Sister Justin fixed each girl with a stare that said she expected the worst and would not tolerate it.

"The girls are on their way downstairs for Mass right now," Sister Christine said.

The five of them bolted, like horses at the starting gate, in a rush for the stairs.

Sister Justin clapped her hands sharply three or four times.

"Young ladies in my charge will not rush about. Come back and stand at the foot of your bed, every one of you."

They scuffed back, abashed and angry.

"And no one will ever leave this dormitory with her bed unmade except for grave emergency. Tidy habits make tidy lives."

Lucy turned furiously and bent over to make her bed. The red hat fell off her head and onto the tangled sheets and she slapped it back on her head. It fell off again. Someone giggled. She flung it on the floor.

"We'll have no childish displays. Pick up that hat and hand it to me. I'll hold it while you finish making the bed."

Lucy picked up the hat, held it toward Sister Justin's outstretched hand, and dropped it as though it were contaminated. Sister looked at her with a slight pale smile.

"I can see that we're going to have to work very hard on graceful conduct. One's deportment tells a great deal about one's inner condition. Now finish up that bed and we'll all go to the chapel. Like the ladies we are."

Sister Justin stood perfectly still, holding the hat as

though it were some sort of measuring device, while Lucy struggled awkwardly with the sheets. Everyone had become suddenly silent, watching her. She finished, fuming, tucked the spread up around the plump pillow, and turned to Sister Justin for the hat. Sister handed it to her, the small fixed smile on her lips.

"At Mass this morning let us all ask God's blessing on the endeavors we will begin together today."

Out of the corner of her eye, Lucy could see Joanne's face narrowing. It was as though Joanne were slipping on a second skin, an impenetrable armor against whatever barbs might be directed at her. The thought came to Lucy, with a shock of sudden pain, that Joanne would never feel anything. She was impervious to any outrage, anguish, or humiliation that might affect the rest of them. Joanne could pass through fire and flood untouched. She would never be moved, she would never be broken. She would never be loved. Lucy drew her eyes off that closed face with horror. It was better to be hungry, she thought, than to be already dead of starvation. The sweet sense of possibility took hold of her. She fastened on it greedily. To be aware of that was no small thing. She put on the hat without resentment and walked, with a feeling of grace, to the chapel.

## Chapter 6

It was hard to hold on to that feeling in the next few weeks. Sister Justin, with her pale, wintery smile, her unyielding insistence on routines, her constantly invoked and seemingly inexhaustible store of moral mottoes, checked every impulse toward delight, joy, activity. The five girls submitted to her presence, her order of existence, with a kind of dull quiescence.

Sister Justin, it seemed, was always there. Mealtimes, when before they had exchanged insults, quarreled, battled for position, aligned against one another, or allied in some rare common cause, were a different affair now. The two tables had been pushed against one another. They all sat together. They ate in silence, with Sister

Justin reading aloud from dull novels, books of poetry, essays on the spiritual life. From time to time she would interject a corrective remark on table manners in the midst of her reading without breaking stride, without altering the high, metallic tone of her voice.

"So that at the same moment we rejoice in His coming for the salvation of men, the knife is laid across the top of the plate after cutting meat, and it is laid soundlessly, and offer again to God His Body and Blood in sacrifice, oblation and satisfaction for the sins of the world."

Sister Justin, through it all, seemingly never looked up from the book she was holding. Once Carol had spilled half a ladle of gravy on the checkered tablecloth, and without pausing in the poem she was reading to them, Sister Justin had moved to Carol's place, reached into her pocket, and produced a huge muslin handkerchief which she held out to Carol. Carol took it wordlessly, blotted up the puddle of gravy, and put the balled-up handkerchief back into the outstretched hand like someone drugged. Sister Justin replaced the damp, wadded square somewhere in her skirt, turned the page and went on reading. They were all struck dumb by the imperturbable, dead efficiency of it. Not one dared a smile.

In the evenings, after dinner, she sat on a small straight-backed chair in the dormitory darning the heels of her thick black stockings, sliding the polished wooden egg up to the worn-through heel or toe, needling in and out, up, down, and around the hole until it disappeared. From this position of minor enthronement, she would direct their study period with the same unerring aptitude for singling out the girl whose attention had lapsed from her books.

"Carol, read aloud the paragraph you're considering at

the moment in your American history text, please." The eyes continued to fix on the sliver of steel working its correction on the black stockings.

"Joanne, stop studying your nails. They won't be of any help tomorrow in your typing-speed drill. Idle hands are the devil's workshop."

"Virginia, sit down and apply yourself. A third trip to the bathroom in less than an hour isn't necessary. Or, if it is, let me know in private, and I'll arrange for a consultation with the doctor."

They were all uncomfortable about what was happening between Sister Justin and Ginny. The second night Sister was with them, she noticed the single, small slice of roast beef on Ginny's dinner plate. Ginny was cutting it meticulously into tiny strips and chewing each strip in the slow, deliberate fashion that she had adopted since she had begun dieting. They had all mocked her, tormented her when she began, but the gradual, visible results earned everyone's admiration. Ginny's clothes hung loose and slack on her. Her skirts were all belted in thick tucks about her waist; her blouses and sweaters seemed huge and ludicrous across her shoulders, which had lost their plumpness. Her face, which had been the first to register the weight loss, was showing fine, tiny features, and delicate high cheekbone began to emerge where there had been rosy-apple roundness. Ginny was waiting patiently for the switch from winter to summer clothes when she would blossom forth from the woolen cocoon, and wear a bathing suit without humiliation. They had seen it happen and, in some secret fashion, it was everyone's triumph.

Sister Justin saw nothing but the dinner plate.

"Virginia, kindly serve yourself an adequate portion of all the foods on the table," Sister Justin said.

"I'm on a diet, Sister."

"All of us are on a diet—a diet balanced to meet our nutritional needs."

Ginny threw an anguished glance around the table, but the rest of them were studiously attacking mounds of mashed potatoes and succotash. She dropped a dab of each onto her plate and sat regarding them miserably.

"Adequate, adequate," Sister Justin said softly, unyieldingly, and taking up the serving dishes, she filled Ginny's plate. Ginny's face worked visibly in the struggle. She loved succotash. They used to call her "the lima-bean fiend" when she would return for a third, even fourth helping if it were available. The mashed potatoes were fragrant and white. All through them, little hidden pockets of butter were ready to break into golden veins of flavor at the touch of a fork. She sighed deeply and began eating with the old vigor. Under Sister Justin's cool, unpleasured presence, she began to eat recklessly, and food had never seemed so delicious. The breads that Sister Gratia baked every day in the kitchen came up with the warmth of the oven all fresh about them. New potatoes came into season, their delicate nutty flavor a meal in itself. Vegetables were fresh from the market; she celebrated the flavor of each with large doses of butter. By the middle of the second week Ginny had gained seven pounds.

Then Lucy had discovered what Ginny was doing. She had gone into the bathroom after dinner to brush her teeth, and heard the sounds of gagging from behind one of the closed toilet doors.

"Ginny, is that you?"

The answer came after a sequence of strangled sounds. "It's not your grandmother's ghost."

"What's the matter? Are you sick? Should I get Sister?"

"All I'm sick of is her cramming me full of food I don't want but can't help eating."

Ginny flushed the toilet and came out, her eyes watery and red-looking, the faint curl of nausea still flickering about her mouth. She marched to the washbowl and scrubbed her hands with surgical thoroughness, then washed and dried her face.

"D'you mean eating your dinner makes you sick?" Lucy asked, amazed, still not understanding what Ginny was telling her.

"I make myself sick. See?" She opened her mouth and wiggled two fingers in mid-air demonstratively. "Remember the Romans?"

Lucy twisted her head away from the sight of Ginny in a spontaneous motion of revulsion. "Oh, Ginny, that's disgusting. Oh, don't even tell me about it!"

"Well, you've been told. I'm sorry, but that's the way it is." Ginny's voice had a belligerent tone that was completely alien to her.

"Why don't you just go to Sister Christine? I mean, she's not a complete idiot like some of the others around here. She'd tell Sister Justin not to make you eat so much."

"Listen, Lucy, I'm not going to anyone for anything any more." For just a minute Lucy heard the pleading edge, the thread of heartbreak in Ginny's voice. It was only there for an instant; then she was speaking in the new, firm voice that was so strange and so impressive a cry for survival. "I'm looking after myself from now on. I'm doing things my own way. If I'm wrong, it's *me* that's wrong; if I come up with something good, it's *mine*. I'm not blaming anybody, and I'm not asking anybody for any favors. Maybe I'm taking a chance, but that's better than waiting for one. I'm sick of little fat Ginny. I want something else, and I swear to you, I'll get it. And I'm not asking you to help me, Lucy. I'm just asking you to leave me alone. I'm asking you not to go blabbing."

"I think you're nuts," Lucy said, after Ginny's outburst. "But around here, who isn't? I won't say a word."

And she hadn't. But, somehow, all of them had apparently discovered what Ginny was doing. Every evening, after the dinner dishes had gone downstairs and Sister Justin set the girls to supervised study, they would glance knowingly at one another as Ginny walked deliberately, once, twice, sometimes three times, to the bathroom, set the tap running full force or flushed a toilet to cover the sounds of vomiting. She would return to her study desk, eyes cast down or looking straight ahead, engaging no one's glance of amazement, reproof, or compassion.

Had it not been for Ginny, Lucy felt she might almost enjoy having Sister Justin in charge. There seemed to be more breathing space in the full daily routine; the peace was no less tenuous, but each day of that enforced order strengthened it. Every one of them had improved in schoolwork. There had not been a single quarrel about clothes, because Sister Justin allowed no borrowing, no exchanging. She personally checked each one of them before bedtime to ascertain the condition of underwear, hair, nails, skin for the next day. She had confiscated every item of Joanne's cosmetic arsenal.

"Smooth skin comes from within, not without," she

said. "Eat bananas; the oil in them is good for your complexion." No one ate bananas, but no one argued with her.

Helen followed Sister Justin's directives like someone in a trance. Sister insisted that they spend an hour each evening in concentrated study. Helen spent two. Sister Justin required them to do all their washing and ironing on Saturday morning before they were allowed the freedom of the day. Helen made laundry a daily chore. And when Sister Justin insisted that they learn the basic stitches for working a sampler, telling them that no lady need ever be idle if she learned to be clever with a needle, they had all resisted any attempt to teach them cross-stitching, feather-stitching, simply because Helen had seized upon needle-work as though it would prove to be a singularly redemptive act.

On Sundays, if the girls had no company, Sister Justin sat them down and provided them with "quiet work" if they had none of their own. Helen was working a sampler with dogged determination. Time after time Sister Justin had made her tear out an entire line of work, saying that the stitches were uneven or the threads too loose. "You'll want this to last for more than a lifetime. Good needle-work can be passed on to your children," she said, "if properly done, if properly done."

Helen's sampler had a picture of a mantelpiece with an old clock and vase of flowers on it. Above the mantelpiece were two oval portraits, one of a man, one of a woman, facing each other in benign silhouette. Helen had finished this much, and even Lucy had to admit that it was nicely done. But now she was working the verse underneath, in fine black cross-stitch.

Hours fly,
Flowers die.

New Days,
New Ways

Pass by.
Love stays.

Sunday after Sunday, Sister Justin had made Helen tear out that final line, laboriously completed: *Love stays.*

Lucy couldn't bear to watch it any more. She had begun a sampler herself, bearing the legend, "Enough is as good as a feast." Sister Justin had never let her get past "Enough."

The days were cold and dreary, making a liar out of the calendar, which said it was April. Carol, checking the dates, reminded Lucy that Sister Justin had arrived on the first of the month. "A great April fool's joke," she said.

Carol had submitted, with the rest of them, to the required lessons in needlework, doing her sample stitches in the piece of white sheeting that Sister Justin had provided, but she had refused when Sister unrolled the pack of samplers with mottoes printed on them for those who wanted to choose one for themselves.

"No, thank you, Sister," Carol murmured with new politeness. "I want to finish repairing a piece of china first." And she had taken the Delft shoe from Lucy, saying, "I'm tired of doing things I *have* to do. Let me fix this for you."

Ginny had joined forces with Carol, the two heads, one fair, one dark, bent over a table by the window of the dormitory. Their hands trembling sometimes at the precision of the task, they had spent two weeks watching the late-afternoon sun melt weakly into dusk as they pieced and patched the shoe. It had become as obsessive for them as the sampler had become for Helen. It was finished now, but Lucy, strangely, attached no more importance to the shoe. She passed those quiet hours devouring *Jane Eyre* and *Wuthering Heights*.

Sister Justin had taken away every one of her paperback mysteries, saying that she would replace Lucy's library, volume for volume, with things worth reading. Lucy had almost choked with rage at the unfairness of it, but Sister Justin was adamant. "You'll learn nothing from that peck of trash," she said, tucking at least fifteen of the small books along her thin arm as though it were a wooden shelf. She disappeared into her cubicle and returned with a handsomely bound copy of *Jane Eyre*. "You're just the right age for this. You may keep it for your own. And let me know when you've finished. I'll give you another."

"But, Sister, those were *my* books."

"They're mine now."

"But that's not fair," Lucy insisted stubbornly.

"Fair is a good word for describing weather, or color of skin or hair. It's not a good word to use when describing life, or the process of growing up."

Lucy looked away from the gray eyes that glittered at her from behind polished lenses. "When you've read an equivalent number of the books I will supply you with, you may decide it's been a more than fair exchange, or you may return them all and have the others back if you so choose." Sister Justin smiled grimly and left Lucy full of angry resentment. She would never read one of them, she decided.

But Sister Justin had her way. Faced with a bleak Sunday afternoon alternative of needlework or reading, Lucy had begun *Jane Eyre*. The opening pages won her completely, with their mood of raw weather, loneliness, and sore human relationship. Her heart flooded with pity for Jane, so much, she thought, like herself. She wept and triumphed with her first real heroine, supplying in full all the compassion and understanding that Jane missed from her world. And Mr. Rochester—Lucy brooded about him for days, imagining how easily she would be able to love a man like that.

Joanne, whose mother visited each Sunday as unfailingly as night followed day, would come in afterward and regard the other four, bent quietly over their work, like a visitor from a far country.

"What creeps," was her usual greeting. They were all beginning to look at Joanne now as somehow harsh and glaring. "Charlene says I look like hell," she announced to them triumphantly, the first Sunday after Sister Justin had taken her cosmetics away.

"I think you look a lot better, if you want my opinion," Carol said.

"Well, you can have your opinion. I *don't* want it. All I want is to get out of this dump. Charlene says she's taking me home this summer."

"Home?" They all dropped whatever they were doing and lifted their eyes at the word.

"Where's home?"

"Well, there's *going* to be one. Charlene's moving—getting a regular house, probably—she's quitting at the club if . . ." Joanne stubbornly closed off the flow of talk, but they pressed her for information hungrily.

"Well, she's getting married again," Joanne said sullenly.

"You're kidding."

"I'm not. And she's not. I just hope he's not."

"Who is he? Have you met him?"

"Yeah. He's a drummer at the club." Joanne began snapping, rhythmic noises with her fingers. Her body loosened and she gyrated around the floor. Her hips shivered nervously out of context with the rest of her body. Her eyes took on a narrow, glazed look. She stopped suddenly, as if remembering something, and smiled to herself. "He thinks I'm cute," she said.

Sister Justin came into the dormitory then and Lucy was amazed at the relief she felt. Joanne's nightclub dancers and drummers had threatened her; they had no place in her scheme of things. She was grateful for the dull reading at dinner that night. She went to bed early, with the sense of something about to happen.

First came the two days of rain. Dark skies hung low and gray over the stone buildings of St. Michael's. Day and night there was the hypnotic sound of rain on the roof. Gutters flooded; boots, clogged with mud, were lined up against the wall in the front vestibule on a wide plastic runner out for the duration of the weather. Sister Christine doled out raincoats which seemed too large or too small for most of them. They set out those mornings for their various schools in straggling groups of half a dozen or more to catch buses on Summit Street, the younger girls dragging plastic book bags close to the wet pavement, the older girls hunched protectively over books and brown-paper lunch bags. Noses ran, curled hair hung in limp fishhooks, classroom lights were on all day. The second night there was a terrific thunderstorm.

Lucy came wide awake, startled out of her sleep by an explosion of thunder. She tunneled further under the blankets, waiting for the next sound, thinking how long it had been since the last spring rain. Lightning seamed the sky briefly, throwing sudden shadowy shapes against the walls of the dark dormitory. She heard the padded sound of half-running unshod steps and knew, before looking, that it would be Marcella.

"Marcella, what are you doing up here? You know Sister . . ."

"Come to the window and watch the storm with me."

"I can't, Marcella. You know the rules."

"But the rules don't know me. Oh, come on, Lucy. All day, all week, probably for a year I've been waiting for something to happen. I can feel it coming, it's so close. Maybe it's a message. Maybe there's going to be a message written in the sky for me." She reached out a pale white hand in the dark and touched Lucy imploringly, laying her fingers between Lucy's shoulder blades. Lucy pressed back her shoulders involuntarily, and the blades of bones stretched the skin tight.

"Oh, Lucy, you're sprouting wings." Marcella laughed a weird, whispering kind of laugh. "You're going to be an angel. Or else a hunchback." She smiled, the room flashed light, then dark over her face. She rubbed Lucy's shoulder blades reflectively. "When do you think I'll get breasts?"

"What?"

"Breasts. You know. When do you think I'll grow up?"

Lucy sighed, "When it's time for you to," she said sadly, tenderly.

"I want to grow up, Lucy, but I know I never will."

"Don't be silly—everybody does."

"Ah, now you're being silly—almost nobody does. At least nobody I know ever did. Mamma didn't. Mamma's a baby." She giggled at the thought, trying to muffle the noise, so that it came out in short hissing darts of sound. "You know, if I find out I'm not growing up, I'll have to do something about it."

"Oh?"

"Well, of course I'd have to. I don't know—if I didn't just die in time, I guess I'd have to hide somewhere—what would you do?"

"I think I'd just try to grow up," Lucy said dryly.

"But I don't think you ought to have to *try*. It ought to just happen. Everybody is always *trying* so hard on everything. Why can't they let things *be?*"

"Because things aren't the way they ought to be."

"That's what everybody says. But who's ever given it a fair chance? Every wrong thing I've ever seen comes from people trying to change, rearrange, fix things up the way they want it for themselves. It must have started a million years ago, because I can't even imagine the beginning."

"Nobody can, I guess," Lucy said. She felt, for the moment, that she might be a million years old herself. "So there's nothing to do but make your own beginning. Each person *must* have to be his own beginning. It's the only way to make sense out of it."

"There you go. Just like the rest of the world. Trying to make sense out of it. Maybe there isn't any sense in it. Or maybe we just don't get it. Anyway, I'm not going to run around looking for reasons. I'd rather look at storms." She left Lucy's bed and walked to the window. All around them it was dark. From time to time there would be a brief arc of charged light, showing them forms, shapes, disappearing before they had time to discover any pattern, detail. After each report of thunder there would be the sounds of heavy breathing, troubled sleep. Once someone cried out, "No—Mother." The voice was drugged with sleep and Lucy had no idea which one of them had spoken. She went from her bed to the window and stood beside Marcella.

Marcella was standing, feet planted apart, her chin slightly lifted, her eyes fixed on the small rivers of rain that branched out against the pane of glass. Every few minutes a gust of wind would blow up against the window, spreading the streams into a flat sheet of moisture, which would shiver off again into thin trickling traces. Once in a long succession of lightnings, she turned to look at Marcella. The pattern of rain on the window had somehow been cast off, reflected as it were, onto Marcella, giving her the momentary look of a face, a figure completely punished with tears. It was as though her entire body were weeping.

Lucy put her arm around her sister's shoulders then and sensed how frail, how foolish, really, the body was to house the spirit.

"It shines through like treasure in a thin paper bag, doesn't it?" Marcella said, looking at the lightning.

Lucy trembled at the words. "Marcella, you scare me," she said. "Go on back to bed."

"I don't mean to," Marcella said. "You're shivering, Lucy, and it's not cold. *You* go back to bed. And I will too," she added. "I'll even tuck you in." Her face flowered into a smile and she took Lucy's hand and led her back to bed like a child, pulling the blankets up over her.

"Good night, Lucy." She was halfway across the dormitory when she turned, came back, and looking gravely down at Lucy, said, "You be the beginning, Lucy, and I'll be the ending." Then she was gone.

## Chapter 7

And the next day it was spring. It had come that suddenly, happening overnight as snow will sometimes happen, changing the world about them so certainly that they could not really remember what it had been like only a day before. The trees all showed a fine tracery of green along their branches and drops of rain still clung to the new lacy edge of things, glittering in the morning light. Squirrels on the lawn raced madly about, chasing one another in an excess of energy. The statue of Christ thrust its arms forth strongly, tenderly, as though feeling, embracing, bestowing, all in the same single gesture, this gift of the new season. Sister Justin had opened the windows and sounds drifted in. The far-off murmur of traffic on

Summit Street, the clarion call of an occasional automobile horn, the soft joyous conversation of two of the younger girls who had somehow stolen outside before breakfast for a taste of the new day, and everywhere an entire creation of birds, it seemed, calling to one another in the soft cleansed air about them—all of it filled Lucy with such a sense of praise that she wanted to sing, cry, laugh out loud, throw her arms around Sister Justin and kiss that pale, stern face just to test the new feeling to its outermost limit.

The new weather affected them all; there was a climate of dreamy restlessness even in the littlest children. The smallest ones played outdoors after school, taking dolls and tiny dishes down to the back of the property where an old roofed pavillion with crumbling, rusty screens and dusty benches flowered to life with their games and songs and pretendings. It always pained Lucy, like an unexpected touch to a forgotten bruise, to hear the smallest ones playing house there, still capable of saying, "You be the father, I'll be the mother," then setting about the business of scolding, praising, imposing order on their mythical families.

Watching from her dormitory window, Lucy noticed that Marcella was at the pavillion almost every afternoon, stationing herself out of sight but still in hearing range, behind a cluster of bushes by the stairs, where she would sit with a lap full of dandelions, daisies, wild honeysuckle, making chains, wreaths, garlands for her neck, her hair, her wrists. Lucy walked down to tell her something one afternoon, smelling the freshness of just-cut grass all about, squinting a little at the late-afternoon sun that still slanted against the end of the property even though the front of the house was already in shade. Marcella did not hear her coming. She was linking a dandelion chain around her wrist, fitting the smaller end into the larger opening of the pale green, hollow stem. Lucy could hear her singing mournfully to herself. Lucy stopped, not wanting Marcella to know she was there, not wanting to miss the words of the strange new tune Marcella was singing. "Woe is me, I'm like a flower, Beautiful now and dead in an hour." Marcella chanted the words over and over, changing the rhythm to suit the pace of the work that engaged her fingers, slowing the song when the stem of a daisy broke or the petals of a honeysuckle branch scattered off unexpectedly, quickening the song until it sounded nearly cheerful as she plaited three strands of a thin trailing vine into a long unbroken braid of fresh green leaves. Lucy turned quietly away and left Marcella alone without remembering what she had come to say to her.

She met Sister Christine on her way back to the house. It struck Lucy that she had not seen Sister, really seen her, for weeks. When Sister Marian had been with them, Sister Christine was in and out of their dormitory, their dining room, their lounge, almost every day. She had been a sort of secondary figure in the daily arrangement of their affairs, consulting, advising, supporting Sister Marian, frequently taking the five of them to her office to insist they cooperate on some point that had thrown Sister Marian into despair.

"Hello, Lucy." Sister had seen her coming up from the pavillion, probably had seen her going to Marcella and sneaking off without a word, and now she was waiting for Lucy to catch up with her on the gravel path.

"Hello, Sister."

Sister Christine began walking as soon as Lucy was beside her. Lucy felt glad of it; she was relieved of the necessity of avoiding Sister's face or smiling a foolish smile she wouldn't really mean.

"Lucy, how happy are you to stay here at St. Michael's?"

The question caught her completely off guard. She felt herself glance sharply, against her will, at Sister's face, to discover there what question it was that she had really been asked. Sister Christine's expression, calm, intelligent, detached, told her nothing.

"What do you mean, Sister?"

"You've been with us for eight years, Lucy."

"It wasn't my idea," Lucy said, surprised at the acid tone in her own voice.

She found herself battling against a crowd of memories. That terrible first night, nine years old and relieved, in the midst of terror, that someone had finally come to take care of the baby for her. She had not gone to school for two weeks, because there was no one to feed Marcella, dress her, keep her away from Mamma, who had never left the kitchen all that time, not even to go to bed. Mamma had slept with her head down on the kitchen table, talking to herself, crying, wringing her hands softly and getting up to walk wretchedly, ineffectually, from stove to refrigerator to closet, moaning as if in pain, refilling her glass from the supply of liquor bottles that seemed to come from nowhere, everywhere. Lucy remembered knocking one of them over trying to open a can of chicken-noodle soup, and Mamma, laughing and crying at the same time, hunching down, her hands with the veins standing out blue on the backs of them, steadying herself against the edge of the table and lapping up the puddle like a thirsty animal. Finally, there had been no more cans of soup, no more clean clothes for the baby. Lucy's third-grade teacher had come to the door that afternoon, and by evening Mamma was in the hospital, Marcella had been taken off, filthy and wailing loudly, by a plump motherly woman who kept crooning, "Poor baby, poor baby." Lucy, frightened and exhausted into docility, had been taken to some office, sat on a chair and given a doll to hold, listened without understanding to a series of phone calls, and finally, believing in the possibility of anything, she had followed a woman to a small black car and been driven to St. Michael's.

She remembered Sister Christine waiting at the front door. It was the first time she had ever been so close to a nun; her knees shook and she answered "Yes, ma'am" to everything. Later that evening, a little girl named Lavinia had told her you called them Sister; and if you weren't good they put you in their convent and dressed you like that and you had to stay for the rest of your life. Lucy didn't remember when she had stopped believing that; she couldn't remember when Lavinia had left St. Michael's. There had been so many girls coming, going, years of them—they filed through her mind now in a long procession of flickering faces, nameless and dreamlike.

Mamma had come home from the hospital, come to St. Michael's to see Lucy, told her she'd bring her back home "as soon as I'm a little stronger." And somewhere in those eight years, Lucy had come to realize that Mamma would always be weak and it was easier with Mamma when you stopped asking the question.

She remembered the day Marcella had arrived at St. Michael's. It was the nearest thing to a family celebration Lucy could remember. Marcella had been at another home, "the baby home," they called it, where all the children were not yet six years old, where everything was miniature and even the toilets were tiny. Lucy had been taken there from time to time by a social worker. It was a long drive, out into the country, and she had loved the trip, with green fields dotted with cows and horses flashing by the window of the car, as much as she had loved seeing her sister. Marcella had never forgotten her. The first time she had gone to visit Marcella, a flock of little faces pressed in around Lucy and the social worker as they walked down the broad, tree-shaded front path to where a group of children were playing in a sandbox. The children had seen them coming, rushed toward them, taken their hands, lifted tiny arms to be picked up, and asked, with a dozen voices that blended into one childish appeal, "Are you my mommy?" And Lucy remembered Marcella, that first time, standing just a little apart from all of them and saying stoutly, serenely, "She's my sister, so she's *my* mommy."

And when Marcella was six years old and able to move to St. Michael's, Lucy was still her mother, for Mamma had never gone to see her at the baby home. Mamma began by saying the trip was too long, her nerves couldn't take it, it could do the baby no good. These excuses had gradually, imperceptibly shifted until Mamma was saying that God was punishing her by taking her baby away from her, the social workers had hatched a plot against her. And now Mamma depended on Lucy for news of Marcella, for Mamma would not come to St. Michael's any more, and home visits were infrequent and allowed only to the older girls.

It had all, all of it, shifted imperceptibly. Mamma and

her house on Franklin Street were the strange world now. The nuns were, after all, only people. The shame Lucy had felt at first, going off to school, feeling sure that everyone knew she lived in a Home for Orphaned and Destitute Children, changed to the occasional twinge of awareness that a man must feel who has learned to see with one eye missing, when he discovers himself being stared at, and suddenly remembers why. Lucy had learned to live with it all. The last real anguish had been having a nun introduce her to her first brassière. But that had been years ago, and the nun was gone now from St. Michael's, and Lucy had been moved from the pre-teens to the upstairs dormitory shortly after the episode.

And now Sister Christine, the one person who had seen her through it all, who must be remembering much of it with her at this very moment, was asking her how happy she was to stay here at St. Michael's.

"What does it matter how happy I am here? I have nowhere else to go. I don't really remember what it was like before." She spoke without bitterness. She felt there was no one to blame, no one to praise, for anything. Whatever might matter lay either too far behind or impossibly out of reach.

"You can't stay here forever, Lucy." They had passed out of the warm sun, into the shade of the east wall. Lucy pressed her hand against the rough gray stone and felt it still giving off warmth from the earlier hours of sun. "You'll be eighteen next year, finished high school." Sister Christine smiled wistfully. "We have to push our birds out of the nest then, whether or not they're ready to fly." They walked in silence a dozen steps or more.

"I think I'll be okay, Sister." She remembered Marcella's remark the night of the storm. "I'm beginning to feel my wings already."

"I think perhaps it's time for you to try them," Sister said.

Lucy felt her heart suddenly quicken. "What do you mean?"

"Lucy, you're one of the very few lucky ones. No, don't stop me," she hurried with an impatient flicker of her hand, on seeing the ironic glitter that flashed into Lucy's eyes at the remark. "Every one here has been hurt; you know that as well as I do. Not one child here has crossed the doorsill without more pain and loss than most people suffer in a lifetime."

"Oh, Sister, skip the commercial, I've heard it before," Lucy said angrily. "I get so tired of the crippled bit. Isn't it enough to live with it all around you? What good does it do to talk about it? I'd like to try, just once, walking without the crutches."

"And that's why you're one of the lucky ones," Sister said quietly. "Lucy, I want to see you try. I'd like you to think about living in a foster home—a real home with real people and real problems. I think you've outgrown us here; it happens so rarely that I find myself six months behind the signs. Sister Justin feels quite positive about you . . . Look here, the jonquils have already had their season," Sister Christine said abruptly, turning her attention to a clump of yellow blooms. The crisp fluted edges of the petals were beginning to wilt around the outer rim, curling under themselves. Some of the stiff green stems and leaves had already drooped. "Think about it, Lucy, and come to see me when you think you have something to say.

I'll be waiting for you." She turned away suddenly and walked to the house.

"Thank you, Sister," Lucy said. But Sister Christine was already out of earshot, or seemed to be, giving no indication of having heard Lucy. Lucy didn't care. She didn't know what she was saying thank you for. Thank you for telling me my days are numbered? For telling me I'm not quite as bad as the rest? For telling me that maybe, maybe, I have a one in a million chance of making it? Lucy walked on by herself, not wanting to go back inside just yet. Her thoughts were tangled in a maze of sudden feeling for St. Michael's. A real home, Sister Christine had said, with real people and real problems. But what was a real home? Having a room to yourself, maybe, and being able to do things alone, without half a dozen girls wanting to join you or, worse still, trying to spoil your plans. Being able to fix your own breakfast, sleep late on Saturdays, read the papers on Sunday in a living room instead of a lounge, using a bathroom whose single toilet, sink, and tub would constitute a kind of luxury in itself. It all struck Lucy as false. She could not imagine herself away from the high ceilings she had closed her eyes against so many times, lying on her back, trying to stay awake, trying to sleep; the polished wooden floors that had echoed so often with her angry steps. She could never leave the wide green lawns, the gravel paths that wound about the property, took you back to the toolsheds, down to the pavillion, on to the statue of Christ, and back to the broad front stairs. She could never do without the constant clatter of tongues, the certain circular nature of each day, each week, each month. She stood still and closed her eyes, trying to imagine an existence that led out to something, not back into itself. It was impossible. Everything she thought of turned back to St. Michael's. The faces, the sounds, even the familiar smells of the place possessed her. She felt herself swaying and opened her eyes. Christ was there, turned to stone on the lawn. "Help me," she said softly, under her breath. "Help me, help me learn to say goodbye."

She went into the house, which seemed cool, dim, and comforting, and climbed the wooden stairs to the top floor. The other four were there, sitting cross-legged at the end of the dormitory talking together in a small circle. She didn't know what they were talking about; she knew it wouldn't matter.

None of them would be telling the other anything. They were all strangers, they were all in disguise. It would never be any different here. The pity of it clung to her as a physical feeling, tightening her face, constricting her throat. Helen, so frightened by her plainness; Carol, so frightened by her beauty; Joanne, so sure that everything she had ever done was right; and Ginny, certain that everything she had ever done was wrong—Lucy looked at them all, huddled together as if for comfort. She was filled with loathing and with love for each of them. She felt as if she were seeing those faces, all dreadful and incredibly dear, for the first and last time. There was no place for her in that circle, no way to make room. She knew, with certainty, that she would have to leave them and that there was not even the possibility of a farewell among strangers.

Ginny saw Lucy first and beckoned her to the group. "Guess what we're talking about," she said. "Boys."

"So what's new?" Lucy said.

"The boys, dear, the boys are new," said Joanne with weary impatience.

"What are they?" Lucy asked, sensing herself the outsider.

"Oh, we don't know them yet, we're just pretending; it's better that way," Carol said. Lucy felt herself blushing before she saw the full, almost angry-looking flush on Carol's face. "Well, you don't have to look so superior about it, Lucy, I don't notice any parade of dates serenading you under the window."

"I didn't ask to join this conversation," Lucy said coldly, "and the more I hear of it, the more I'm glad I didn't. Imaginary boys! Now I've heard everything." She began to walk away from them, when Helen called out, "And of course you don't plan to go with us to the imaginary yacht club on Saturday."

"Is somebody going to tell me what's going on here?" Lucy asked plaintively. The authenticity of Helen's sarcasm told her she had missed some piece of hard information that bound the rest of them together. She felt the lack of that bond, however frail.

"Sister Justin just left," Ginny said. "She waited for you for nearly an hour."

"I was out," Lucy said vaguely, defending her conversation with Sister Christine from them.

"So we noticed," Joanne said. "What's she trying to do? Get you to join the convent?"

"What are you talking about?" Lucy asked angrily, knowing that they had seen her from the window. She felt injured, spied upon, cheated by the permanent impossibility of privacy.

"Oh, come on, let's not fight," Ginny said. She edged closer to Carol, drawing up her knees to make room for Lucy. "We're going to the yacht club on Saturday, all of us. Sister Justin just told us."

"Who's taking us?" Lucy asked. She hunched her shoulders and tried to fit into the circle.

"I don't know—there's going to be a bus from here to there, we're having lunch there, we can swim, we're even going for a cruise on a yacht. And Sister Christine is letting us all go downtown this week to buy new bathing suits. I'm so excited I could die."

"I don't believe it," Lucy said, stirred by the desire for some splendid episode. "I've lived here for eight years and nothing like this has *ever* happened. The yacht club? Are you sure?"

"Positive," they answered in unison, a chorus of four, and after a split second of amazement at having all said exactly the same word at the same time, they began laughing together. For one aching moment, Lucy felt dreadfully lonely.

"But who's taking us?" she persisted.

"Oh, I don't know—some group or other, Lions, or Elks, or Moose, I don't know . . ."

"Are you sure it's not the zoo we're going to?" Lucy asked.

They laughed at that too, and Lucy felt one of them again. She joined their talk, fed the conversation with real and invented pieces of information about yachts and yachting. Whenever she sensed the slightest hint of suspicion or resentment in the face of one or the remark of another, she deftly drew the flow of talk back to some point where she could be the questioner, the other person the expert. She grew lighthearted, gay from the grace of being in control. Knowing the depth and limit of each of them, manipulating the four others to a pleasant peace without their even realizing what she was about, filled Lucy with a comforting sense of quiet success and triumph. She knew her place here; all the moves were memorized. She could play her part blindfolded and still come out on top. The idea of leaving them, which she had so freshly formulated, so recently resolved, seemed suddenly far off and ridiculous. That would come of its own accord, and very soon, at that.

One more year here. One more year. It didn't seem long enough; she felt the gnawing anxiety of something that must be done without enough time to finish. "Oh, I couldn't leave here now," she thought, filled with a sense of urgent anguish.

She tried to imagine the unknown foster home. A host of wild, horrible possibilities buzzed in her mind like flies. Who would want her, anyhow? Whoever they were, they'd be sure to change their minds. Or she would hate them. The foster mother might be fat, enormously fat and affectionate, wanting to put her arms around Lucy, wanting to press her against a huge moist bosom. Lucy shrank from the mere thought of that contact. In her mind she was already busy avoiding encounters with this creature. Or the foster father would have dirty fingernails, or hair growing out of his nostrils, or he would scratch his stomach after a big meal and loosen his belt at the table. Now she saw him taking his shoes off in the living room and massaging between his toes, with thick black socks still on his feet. Ah, she loathed him. She would never put herself in the position of having to live with such people. The world was full of them. They crawled on the surface of everything, like bugs, incapable of being anything but the ugly, harmless, toiling creatures they were by nature; unaware, even, of how the mere sight of them could make your flesh crawl. Why was it that people grew up to be like that? You saw them everywhere, on buses, on street corners, at lunch counters, in downtown stores, sitting on benches in the park in warm weather like lumps of dough set out in the sun to rise. And she supposed they must all live in homes, "real homes," Sister Christine had called them. "I'll not go," Lucy thought fiercely, sickened by the train of thought she had begun, by the series of vivid imaginings that would not leave her alone now, but continued to surround her, suffocate her spirit, feeding on her recent sense of purpose, slowly, surely, with blind tenacious mouths.

# Chapter 8

"Here it is! The bus! The bus is here!" You could hear the shouts of excitement all over the house, the scramble to gather up beach bags, the sudden cries of panic, "Sister, I can't find my bathing suit," the whispery giggles of the younger girls as they lifted up their skirts to assure one another that they were really being allowed to wear shorts when they got there, even though Sister Christine had insisted that they wear skirts over them, coming and going. "And I won't be replacing any skirts that don't find their way back home," Sister had cautioned. "Anyone who loses a skirt will just have one less skirt for summer."

Lucy slid her bare feet into a pair of tan leather sandals, admiring the tiny gold buckle that glinted on her instep.

She loved the untarnished look of the small sandal fastening, loved the clean feel of any new thing. She knew that there were people who never felt comfortable in a dress, a hat, a pair of shoes, until they had worn them often enough to have obscured just that quality she found so attractive, so dear in its sense of freshness. She tried but could not understand that sort of person. She slung her bag over her shoulder and hurried downstairs.

The pale flash of bare arms and legs churned the huge front hall into a sea of activity. The younger girls maneuvered back and forth, jockeying for position with an older favorite. "Can I sit with you?" "Will you teach me to swim?" "Are there spiders or snakes at a yacht club?" "When you get a sunburn, do you peel?" "How does it feel to be on a boat?" Lucy listened to the questions, heard the pitch of excitement that made any answer impossible, and knew that none of them really cared about anything but the sense of adventure, the intoxicating possibility of the new day, the new world, that would begin when the door of the huge red and silver bus hissed shut and they sank back into the deep-cushioned obscurity of a plush seat.

None of the nuns were going. They stood back against the walls of the front hall, immobilized by the crush of excitement around them, looking on with a kind of benign detachment. The group of lady chaperones, making helpless efforts to organize the outing, looked somehow foolish in the face of those calm nuns. Lucy knew the ladies were disconcerted by the unfamiliarity of it all. Still, she thought, they could not possibly feel the tenderness, the instant affection for each girl that they were at such pains to demonstrate. They looked so solicitous, so eager to retie a hair ribbon that did not need retying, so sympathetic when someone stepped on someone else's bare toe. Lucy saw how slyly the smallest children inserted themselves into the luxury of this counterfeit feeling. She watched the youngest of them bend down swiftly, deliberately loosening her shoelace, and then scanning the strange faces, she discovered the plumpest, the most obviously corseted lady in the group.

"Will you tie my shoe, please?" she asked with curdling innocence, thrusting the small foot forward, and then looked triumphantly at the rest of the girls over the rounded mountain of flesh that stooped to do her bidding. Lucy met Sister Christine's eyes presiding over the episode. They were cool, intelligent, amused. Lucy smiled in spite of herself. The answering smile from Sister Christine sent a thrill of pleasure through her. It was a private smile, just for Lucy. Lucy never remembered having known such a moment of complete harmony, such a fragile and superb poise of understanding and being understood. It leapt from heart to heart, bound them together, touched her with a keen joy close to pain. It was better than any words; it was like a new way of talking where the wrong thing could never be said. It lasted only an instant, but Lucy felt that smile on her like a blessing as she took two of the small girls by the hand and led them onto the bus.

They left then with cries of "Goodbye" and "God bless you," showering all about them. The bus door clamped shut; the ladies sighed with relief at the temporary respite of traveling time and sank back into their seats. Lucy craned her neck, turning her head for a last glimpse of the nuns together on the front steps. They had already begun scattering, two of them hurrying back inside, half a dozen walking out on the grounds, holding their small black veils at the bottom edge as a gust of sudden breeze swelled them out like tiny, fine black sails. Only Sister Christine and Sister Justin remained on the stairs, looking like figures in a landscape, still as the buildings that backed them, but for the slow waving of pale white hands above the black triangle of skirt. Lucy watched them till the bus turned onto Summit Street and scissored them out of her sight.

She talked to no one, keeping her face toward the window to prevent the possibility of conversation while she examined the feeling that had introduced itself to her so recently. She felt wondrously whole, complete, and yet not full but curiously empty. She seemed to herself a vessel, wonderfully made, finely ornamented, waiting to be filled. It was this sense of perfect emptiness that was so beautiful. She fixed her attention to it, held it in her mind, but lightly. She feared any sudden move, any darting gesture of the will that might startle it off forever.

She was only dimly aware of motion, thinking, as if in some detached corner of her mind, how strange it was that her heart, her lungs, her very bones and veins were moving at the same speed as the bus, while she sat perfectly still. She rode that way for quite a while. Then the bus rumbled to a slow stop. She realized that the streets had widened, the warehouses of the inner city had gradually given way to green fields and the sudden shimmer of water. Then the clatter of tongues broke into Lucy's mind, shrieks, laughs, meaningless chatter, and over it all, the hissing, insistent "Shhh" of a chaperone who stood at the front of the bus holding up two fingers in a ridiculous, impotent gesture for silence, waiting with a patient grieved smile that said, "I'm sorry, but I'll wait all day, if necessary, until every one of you is absolutely quiet."

Lucy knew it would take more than a moment. She looked out the window and saw a thin, nervous man in white tennis shorts trying to look jolly over a gigantic clump of balloons that seemed as if they would lift him off the ground if he added one more to the bunch. He waved at the bus, showed his teeth in a huge forced smile, then bent down to a gas cylinder and began grimly inflating more balloons. Lucy wanted to laugh at him. Then she saw a circle of men, in business suits, not shorts like the balloon man, waving their arms at one another in heated conversation, gesturing toward the bus. One of them shook his head "no" as if his life depended on it. Then, after throwing up his hands in a brief motion of anger, he slid them into his pockets, hunched his shoulders, and walked away. Looking through the space where he had stood, Lucy saw with excitement that they were all surrounding a kind of metal platform on wheels that held what must be a television camera. She heard someone cry, "We're going to be on TV!"

She drew her eyes away from the men to look at the lady in front of the bus. She still stood there, the smile still fixed on her face like a mask that had no meaning, the expression of her eyes asking, triumphantly, Lucy thought, "*Now* will you be quiet?" Everyone understood instantly. Purses snapped open for combs, mirrors, lipsticks for the oldest girls. Lucy felt the pathetic vanity of it but could not stop herself from using the window as a kind of oblique mirror to check on her hair. Outside the window another knot of men, in shorts and sport shirts, came running over to the bus, carrying a huge, furled banner. Lucy saw red, white, and blue lettering on it, but she could not read it. They shouted to one another, "Up a little higher,

Harry," and "Can you get it in the picture as they come off the bus?"

They were all out of their seats now, jamming the aisle with feverish impatience, preening themselves without the slightest trace of self-consciousness. Lucy could feel herself beginning to be embarrassed. She glanced around nervously, guiltily, for Marcella, realizing that she had not seen her, not even thought of her all that day. The lady in front had finally gained her point. They were all quiet, and in the silence Lucy heard her saying, "Now, Marcella, we want you to go off first. Don't even look at the camera, it will be looking at you. And when Mr. Wilson—he's in charge of our outing today—when Mr. Wilson asks you a question, just answer whatever comes to your mind. No need to be nervous. And be *sure* to smile."

Lucy tried to worm her way to the front, to rescue Marcella from Mr. Wilson and his unasked question, but she was pressed back, scolded, "No ugly pushing, please!" by a woman who turned to her companion and murmured, "Beautiful child, beautiful," in the same breath.

No doubt of it, Marcella was a beautiful child, Lucy thought, knowing, not seeing, the mystery of her smile, the eyes full of some enormous tantalizing secret well of joy that always forced a vain inquisitiveness on people when they saw her for the first time. Lucy was not comforted by the thought of Marcella's beauty. She clung to her place in the line of girls with a sense of gloomy foreboding, not allowing herself to imagine what questions, what answers might be formulated out there on that patch of grass she could see lying just out of reach, just a window away.

The line inched forward. Lucy could see out the open front door now. They were talking to Marcella, who stood calmly in the midst of the grinning men with the dignity of a small young queen. She was describing a circle in the air with her hand to emphasize whatever she was saying, and against the background of the other girls, who crowded forward, waving wildly at the cameras, the gesture was invested with incredible grace. Finally Lucy was at the door. She stepped off the bus and heard Marcella saying, "Yes, I've ridden on yachts before; in fact, I've gone around the world on a drop of water." She extended a single finger toward the bus. "Your sign there is only a reminder of where we've all been . . . what we've all lost. It's strange, though, to see you trying to hide your loss by advertising ours. Don't you see how it's all the same thing?" Her smile struck like lightning on the circle of shocked faces.

Lucy stumbled off the bus, wrenching her ankle, casting a wild glance at the huge red, white, and blue banner that ran the length of the bus spelling out ANNUAL ORPHANS' PICNIC. A stabbing pain blazed through her foot, shivered its way up her leg, and lodged in her chest like a stone rolled against her heart. Her face was pasty white, twisted with anguish. She turned it full against the camera that crawled with mechanical eagerness to record the words on the banner.

"You stink; you're rotten and you stink," she said clearly through clenched teeth. Then she took Marcella, still smiling, and led her away from them, dragging her injured foot with all the vengeful fury of a wounded beast.

"Oh, Lucy, you've hurt yourself," Marcella cried, her eyes growing deep with pity.

"Shut up," Lucy said tersely, hobbling along wretchedly, forced into using Marcella for support in spite of herself.

"But, Lucy, just stand here for a minute—no, sit down—let me get somebody to help you, let me tell them . . ."

"Look, Marcella, I want you to stop telling people things. Just stop talking for once in your life. Oh, don't you see," she said, made even more miserable by the sudden look of bewilderment in Marcella's face, "don't you see how they used you out there? Don't you see how they smelled you out, put a string around your neck, and danced you around in front of their camera?"

"I don't know what you mean, Lucy," Marcella said, drawing her fine black eyebrows together in a puzzled expression.

"You don't know what anything means," Lucy answered, hearing a hard edge creeping into her voice, feeling the way her words were taking the shape of a weapon, and unable to stop herself. "You don't know what people are like. You have no idea of how it comforts them to stumble across somebody like you, how they love seeing how normal they are."

"I don't know what you mean, Lucy," Marcella repeated, as though there were no other words left in the world.

"I mean that you shouldn't be allowed out without a keeper. You can't tell the difference between a tiger and an alley cat. You don't even feel it when a pack of them begin gnawing away at you. And I can't hide you behind my back forever, Marcella."

"Oh," Marcella said. She stood quietly for a minute, as though thinking. Her face took on the expression of one trying to remember something far away and forgotten. "Oh," she repeated. She smiled at Lucy, but the light had gone out of her eyes and her face looked as though, somehow, the bones beneath the skin had been quietly dissolved into nothingness. "I'm getting someone to help you anyway," she said softly, and walked away with her chin dropped down nearly to her small, smooth chest.

Lucy could not follow her. She felt weak, sickened with the pain in her ankle. She lowered herself with clumsy care to the grass and examined her foot. It was already swollen and puffed up. The small gold buckle that had pleased her so only an hour ago now cut into the reddening flesh. She loosened it and saw the mark of it pressed into her instep. Beads of sweat broke out on her forehead and upper lip. She wiped them away with the back of her wrist. She had the salty taste of tears in her throat. She wiped at her eyes with the heel of her hand and found them dry. "Good," she said to herself. She had the certain feeling that if she began to cry, for any reason at all, she would never be able to stop. She looked away from her foot, let her eyes wander over the wide, manicured lawns, the clusters of hedge and bush, the big shade trees, and the perimeter of water that were all part of the sure, certain aura of this place. So this was a yacht club, she thought, and people belonged to it; it didn't belong to them, they belonged to it.

She felt the word "belong" grow strange in her mind, as a word often became alien to her when she repeated it over and over. She tried whispering it out loud, to see if the sound of it would restore its sense. The taste of the word was strange on her tongue.

She saw a group of concerned faces hurrying toward her and felt, in spite of herself, the restorative comfort of the rescued. Then a man in tan cotton pants knuckled his knee and bent down to her foot. His fingers were broad, smooth, authoritative as he pressed with gentle insistence along her instep. He cupped the palm of his hand and urged the ball of her foot against it. She saw a feathering of black hairs along the back of his hand, the same black repeated in a stand of fine hairs on his bare forearm. She studied his hand and arm with fascination, isolating it from the rest of him as though it were something detached, flung neatly aside.

She lifted her eyes from his arm to his face, which was serious and kind. He moved her foot from left to right, slightly, exploratively, studying her face as he did it.

"Does this hurt?" It was the first time he had spoken.

"Not really . . ."

"This?"

He repeated the movement in an up-and-down fashion. Lucy sucked in her breath at the pain of it.

"Yes. Ouch, yes," she said, biting her bottom lip for control.

He stopped the movement but did not let go of her foot, continuing to make a cradle of his hand for it.

"I don't think this is anything but a bad sprain," he said to her. "It should be taped, and you'll want to keep off it as much as possible for the next day or so until the swelling goes down." His face was solicitous.

She nodded, feeling something close to disappointment that it was nothing more. She was surprised at wanting to prolong her encounter with this man who could care so for her foot without knowing, without asking anything about the rest of her. He looked back to her foot where it lay in his hand.

"This is Dr. Pelligrini, Lucy," someone said in the interval of silence. It struck Lucy as a completely irrelevant remark, and at the same time she wondered how they knew her name. The doctor looked away briefly from her foot, as though he too considered the introduction an intrusion upon the heart of the matter. She offered a timid smile.

"All the same," he said, as though he had been in conversation with someone, "I think I'd like to have an X-ray just to be certain. No, don't bother," he said, anticipating the arrangements that had not even been mentioned, "I'll drive her over myself; Memorial's not even a mile away. Do you think you can walk with that if I help you?" He angled out his elbow and helped Lucy to her feet. She shifted her weight to her left foot and pulled herself up on the arm he offered her. She could feel the muscles harden with resistance, saw the complete attention in his eyes focused on her until she had gained a tenuous balance.

"Now you stay here and I'll bring my car around. I'll just be a minute."

She watched the back of him walking away, noticed the way he rubbed one elbow reflectively as he walked toward a parking lot, became aware, at that same moment, of an abstract tattoo of freshly cut blades of grass pressed into the side of her leg. She bent over to brush them off, but the unexpected reminder of pain when she forgot to hold her weight back from her foot turned the motion to a desperate clutching reach for the nearest person. Two ladies rushed forward, steadied her, asked her if she had hurt herself. The same question, the same gesture of support that had somehow been so pleasing in the doctor irritated Lucy when it was offered by the ladies. It seemed to her that they were trying to offer her a base copy, a counterfeit coin, trying to purchase by fraud a piece of whatever it was that was so generously given her by Dr. Pelligrini. She drew back from them with distaste, almost comforted by the pain she felt in her foot. The pain was good. It guaranteed the episode as her very own. Far off she could see Joanne and Carol, Helen and Ginny shaking the four corners of a huge cotton blanket and settling it down on the grassy slope. She watched them set themselves out on it, arranging their pale bare arms and legs in the sun. She saw immediately how there would have been no room for one of them if she had been with them, dimly imagined which one would have wandered off in injured silence from the others. She was glad not to be there, glad for this experience that would be her very own. She was so tired of having everything divided by five, or cut into two.

A long black car swung around a circular bed of tulips and eased its way up to the margin of grass. Dr. Pelligrini opened the door on the driver's side, stepped out, and crossed in front of the car to where Lucy stood. He opened the other door and guided her the half dozen steps to the car, offering his arm again as she lowered herself onto the front seat.

"Are you comfortable?" he asked.

She nodded gratefully. He turned to the cluster of men and women already in earnest discussion about lunch and the afternoon cruise.

"I think you can manage without us," he said with a small cryptic smile. He had left his engine running, and when he slid behind the wheel, they were off in the same instant. Lucy liked the way he drove, carefully but without preoccupation. He kept his eyes fixed on the road, but she sensed that his attention was with her.

"Well, you've managed to spoil your holiday," he said

finally when they had left the grounds of the yacht club and were fed into the streams of traffic.

"It doesn't matter," Lucy said.

"What do you mean, it doesn't matter," he said. "Everything matters." She fixed him with surprised eyes. He continued his attention to the road, but she saw that his face was perfectly serious. There was no hint of the amusement she had expected to see around his mouth.

"I guess it does," she said, after a moment of thinking. "I guess everything does matter. I guess what I meant was that I don't care."

"Well, that's different," he said. She waited for him to say more, but he drove along in what struck Lucy as an almost pleased silence.

"Do you know what I mean?" she asked finally, needing to know if he understood.

"I think I do," he said.

"It's not a very comfortable sensation," she said, feeling sorry for herself.

"I'm sure it's not," he said.

"Of course, it's silly for me to even say this to you. It doesn't make any difference to you how I feel," she said.

"Maybe it makes a difference to you to be able to say it to somebody," he said.

"Oh, everything makes a difference to *me*," she said irritably. "What I mind is not making any difference to someone else—*anybody* else. I want to matter to someone other than myself. I don't think that's asking too much, do you?"

"It depends on whom you're asking," he said, and that time he did smile, a smile of unexpected sweetness that made her look away from his face and out the window of the car to where field and tree and bush flashed by and out of sight without asking to be understood.

"And we don't always know when and where we're making a difference," he said.

"Oh, I'm sure I'd know it," Lucy said, turning her face back from the window. "You'd have to know it if you mattered. That's part of mattering."

"Well, maybe it's the knowing you want, even more than making the difference."

"Maybe," she said.

"I'm sure it never occurred to Lucy to know how much she would matter to so many different people, simply because she mattered so much to one."

Lucy frowned. She had lost the sense of what he was saying. He saw her confusion.

"Don't you know the Lucy poems?" he asked.

"*Lucy* poems?" She thought of Marcella and her poems for everybody in the whole world.

" 'She dwelt among the untrodden ways / Beside the springs of Dove, / A maid whom there were none to praise / And very few to love.' "

"Now you're making fun of me," she said.

"Of course I'm not," he said. " 'A violet by a mossy stone / Half hidden from the eye! / —Fair as a star, when only one / Is shining in the sky.' "

"What is this? Did you make up this poem? Why do you call it a Lucy poem?" she said. She was pleased and anxious and confused. It was odd, dreamlike, riding down the highway with a strange man who was a doctor, going to a hospital to see about a twisted foot, and hearing poems recited as though they were everyday conversation.

"Why do you call it a Lucy poem?" she asked again, begged almost, feeling on the verge of something important.

" 'She lived unknown, and few could know / When Lucy ceased to be; / But she is in her grave, and, oh, / The difference to me!' "

"Did you make that up?" Lucy asked again insistently.

"Oh, no." He spoke and drove with the same serious imperturbable assurance. "That was written over a hundred years ago." He smiled.

"But is it really Lucy in the poem, or did you just put my name there?"

"It's really Lucy," he said.

She took a deep breath. "Once, when I was little, I found a bracelet in the gutter. And when I picked it up it had my name on it. It was like a miracle to me then. I thought it must mean something. But I lost it later on. It's funny; I forgot all about that until right now. Your poem reminded me of it."

"It's *your* poem, Lucy. And there are others. You should read them. They've all got your name on them."

He slowed down. Lucy noticed that other cars streaked past them, a momentary whistle of sound, a blob of metallic color. Dr. Pelligrini swung the car off the highway onto a smooth black drive where the only sound was the hard rubber crunch of tire on tar. The air was laced with the smell of lilac bushes—dozens of them—that lined the approach to the hospital. The face of the world had changed again, instantly, totally.

The succession of changes overwhelmed her. What had any one part of it to do with the other? All in one morning: St. Michael's and the yacht club and now this quiet hospital—the nuns, the picnic people, this doctor; she felt that she was outside of herself, a stranger to the girl who sat in the front seat of the car with an injured foot. Neither she nor the girl with the name of Lucy Brannan belonged to any of it. Things happened; they might not mean anything, might never hook up, hinge together, make sense at all unless you got together with the person who was yourself. She found herself watching the stranger who was Lucy Brannan. She felt how the one girl was eating the taste of tears in the back of her throat, saw how her knees shivered, and wondered why they should be shaking so. She felt distracted by the presence of her own body. Her fingers sought business, tucked back a stray strand of her wind-tangled hair, rubbed closed eyelids until bright blue and orange spots appeared before her hooded eyes, and finally, with a sense of relief, she discovered a torn thread of her own skin along the cuticle of her thumbnail. She began deliberately catching at it with the edge of her teeth. It was something she could get hold of.

## Chapter 9

Lucy trailed her finger down the column of P's in the phone book that lay fat and open on her lap. She stopped when a sudden skittering of her heart informed her eye that she had found the right name. Pelligrini, Vincent, M.D., office, 231 S. Lucas, res., 1664 Montrose. She rummaged in the pocket of her shorts for the pencil stub she had brought with her, and copied out the addresses from the listing onto a scrap of paper which she stuffed back into her pocket furtively. She had already decided that if anyone asked her what she was doing, she would say she was looking up the number of a girl she knew from school. But no one even walked by in the hallway. The house seemed deserted. It was a strange time of year at St.

Michael's. It was always this way at the beginning of the summer. You had to find your way around the day all over again. The outside world grew mysterious and blossomed with secret attractions when the trips to and from school, the frail associations with dozens of girls who had nothing to do with St. Michael's, were unhinged from the daily routine.

Someone always told you they were going to call you. And you always believed they would. By the middle of July you would call them. And then someone's mother told you that Susan was away at camp for eight weeks, or that Jane had gone to visit her cousins in California, or that Bob had come by that morning to take Angie swimming for the day at the quarry with the other kids and would you like Angie to phone you that evening when she got home. You always said, that was all right, you'd phone her in a day or two yourself. And you never did. Because you knew that there would be no place, no Bob, no group in the world that would be anything but uncomfortable and embarrassed in the presence of the oddity that was Lucy Brannan who lived at St. Michael's.

And summer was always the season for something uncommon, bizarre, to take place at the Home. You waited for it, watched and prayed for the coming of it that would break the monotony, give you something to talk about. You hunted for signs and stored them in your memory so that you could remind people of how you had known it was going to happen all along.

One summer there had been the man who climbed up the outside fire escape and in through the open bathroom window at three o'clock in the morning. A girl named

Adela had wakened to find him standing over her bed staring down at her. Her screams had roused them all. Sister Christine had flown into the dormitory wearing a long white nightgown. The police had come and taken the man away, locked in unnecessary handcuffs, with a pale sad smile on his face. And then they all remembered having seen the man around the grounds for days before, once with a bundle of garden tools hunched under his arm, once at the front door saying he was from the city water bureau, and had their water been cut off that morning?

Another summer there had been the terrible drowning of the Fitzgibbon twins, Mary and Martha, who had slung their bathing suits over their arms, told Sister Christine to go to hell when she ordered them back upstairs to their dormitory, and then walked out the front door with identical ugly sneers on their wild beautiful faces. They would not be stayed from the swim they had decided upon by "any bossy nun in woolen drawers." Word of the walkout flared up like fire; within half an hour of their departure every girl in the Home had heard of it, was speculating on what punishment they would earn for their insolence. It had been Lucy who said she was betting on Sister Christine to win, and that as far as she was concerned, the Fitzgibbons had spent their last night at St. Michael's. Even now it gave her a chill to think how prophetic her words had been, how dead they had looked in the newspaper photographs where the fires of their flaming red hair had shown dark and quenched by the water that thinned it to snakelike strands about their quiet faces.

The funeral had been from St. Michael's, for the Fitzgibbons' mother had died when they were born, and their father, whom no one had ever seen, was reported in the newspapers as being engaged in missionary activities in some South American village, living on fruit, vegetables, and water, and saying, about the death of his daughters, that God had told him to remain where he was, bringing life to the living, and to let the dead bury their dead.

Lucy went over it all in her mind and allowed herself to wonder for a moment what signal event it might be that would mark out this summer for all the girls at St. Michael's. The futility of the exercise became apparent to her almost instantly, and she shook herself out of the reverie. The paper cover of the phone book was sticking to her skin where she had laid it across her bare knees. A single drop of perspiration gathered in the well at the back of her knee and slid down her leg. She wiped it away, peeled the phone book off, and replaced it on the dark wooden table. She didn't know why she wanted Dr. Pelligrini's address. Her sprained ankle was completely recovered. The anklet of pale skin where the tape had been was scarcely noticeable any more. One more day in the sun would erase even that reminder.

She felt hot, sleepy and hot, and nothing seemed important enough to do.

"Maybe I'll just go upstairs and take a nap," she told herself, feeling vaguely guilty about doing nothing. "I really ought to do something this summer—get a part-time job, study French, maybe make a really good list of books and read them all." She thought immediately of how the last idea would please Sister Justin and she discarded it. "I don't want her thinking she's introduced me to culture," she thought sourly.

It bothered her, pained her almost, each time she had to

go to Sister Justin to get a new book. She felt uncomfortable, oddly humiliated by the chilly pleasure that showed through Sister's face as she questioned Lucy about the book she had just finished, asked her opinion, pointed out things like symbolism or character contrasts that Lucy hadn't noticed. Once, exasperated, Lucy had told Sister Justin she was taking all the pleasure out of reading. "No, dear, I'm teaching you how to put all the pleasure *in* reading," Sister had answered. And Lucy had taken the next book with a mixture of eagerness and disgust.

She longed, at times, to tell Sister she hated the books, to insist, somehow, that they were not books that a seventeen-year-old girl would enjoy reading, to assert the fact of Sister Justin's fallibility. But Sister Justin chose wisely, and Lucy could not deny to herself, though she told it to no one, that the sheer physical fact of the books, cleanly set on heavy quality paper, beautifully bound and lined up, ten in number now, on the shelf above her desk, was a pleasure to her heart.

"I'll get my book and go find a tree to sit under and read," she told herself, feeling cooler and more energetic the minute she decided it. She was hurrying up the stairs to the dormitory when she heard, with annoyance, the familiar sharp clapping together of palms that signaled Sister Justin's presence and displeasure. She stopped on the first landing, looked down to the first floor, where Sister had just stepped out of the nuns' Community Room. Lucy raised her eyebrows to indicate she had heard, but refused to speak first. Sister Justin waited a moment, gathered Lucy's intention, and smiled with maddeningly invincible calm.

"I want to speak to you," Sister said quietly, breaking

the silence, conceding the point and winning the encounter by a significant pause that forced Lucy to come back down the flight of stairs she had just climbed.

"I won't read that book," Lucy vowed to herself, coming down the stairs with elaborate dignity. She noticed, with satisfaction, that when she stood close enough, Sister Justin was forced to look up to her.

"You certainly don't look like a young lady in those . . . trousers," Sister Justin said.

"Sister Christine lets us wear shorts around the house in summer," Lucy answered, making her voice amiable.

"I want you to go upstairs, bathe, and change into something cool and ladylike and fresh," Sister Justin said.

"Are you going to tell me why?" Lucy said with cheerful indifference that she knew would be aggravating.

"Miss Fairfax is coming this afternoon and Sister Christine wants to see you with her at 2:30." Sister Justin ignored the startled look that Lucy flashed at her when she mentioned the name of the social worker. "I'm certain Miss Fairfax will be dressed like a lady," she announced coolly.

"What's this about, Sister?" Lucy asked, forgetting to submerge the anxious curiosity.

"I really can't say, Lucy," Sister Justin answered ambiguously. "But you're certainly in no trouble as far as I'm concerned. Now hurry along and make yourself respectable." She pressed her lower lip into position with her long teeth, hesitated just a moment as though there might be something more she wanted to say, and then disappeared back into the Community Room wordlessly.

Lucy felt suddenly wide awake, quickened by the nervous energy that always lay in wait at the back of your brain, eager to knot your stomach, sweat your armpits, remind you that everything was tenuous. It was not a completely unpleasant sensation, and Lucy found herself curious about the various possibilities of Miss Fairfax's visit.

Maybe it would be the foster home Sister Christine had spoken of; Lucy shuddered with delicious repugnance. Maybe Mamma was in the hospital again; she tried to feel sorry about that but couldn't make it work. Perhaps her father had come to take her and Marcella away to a wonderful life together somewhere. He had a new wife—young and beautiful—and she loved Lucy and Marcella instantly. Her heart ached with pity and compassion for all that the two of them had been through. The notion of Mamma inserted itself into the idyl Lucy was constructing; Mamma would never change, and she had no place in a dream. Lucy dissolved her. But now the edge was off the excitement of pretending; somehow that had all been dissolved along with Mamma.

Lucy went upstairs to the bathroom, fitted the plug into the tub, turned on the water too fast so that it splashed off the white porcelain onto the wall beside the tub. She went to get a clean dress out of her locker.

Helen was alone in the dormitory. Lucy saw, with a rush of discovery and anger, that she was rummaging through the bottom drawer of Lucy's bureau. She did not appear to have heard Lucy in the bathroom. There was nothing hurried or furtive about her motions. She was taking her time over Lucy's private possessions as though they were her own inheritance. The mended Delft shoe, with its varicose tracings of cracks and darkened glue, sat on the cleared surface of Lucy's study desk. An unopened pack of cigarettes and four wrapped pieces of bubble gum lay beside it. A small scattering of cheap jewelry, rings, bracelets, pins in the shapes of animals with pieces of colored glass for eyes, populated the bedspread. Helen was working her way through a pack of holy cards with messages from various nuns inscribed across the backs of them. Beside her foot, on the floor, lay an opened scrapbook filled with newspaper clippings about heroic rescues, community citations for public service, stories of pets who had traveled thousands of miles to find their families after a move, pictures of teenage boys receiving Eagle Scout awards, photographs clipped from magazine ads for shirts, pipe tobacco, life-insurance policies, all of them showing faces of men, young, old, middle-aged, some conventionally handsome, some quite plain, but with a certain engaging quality or intelligence in their expression.

"Get out of my things, you dirty sneak," Lucy said with fury. She strode across the dormitory, meaning to tear the cards from Helen's hand. Helen looked up from the pack of holy cards with mild surprise in her eyes.

"You save everything nice, don't you, Lucy?" she said.

"Don't you know what privacy means?" Lucy said. She stood over Helen. Her anger made her feel taller than she was, but the quiescent posture of Helen, small, legs tucked beneath her, shoulders rounded and thrust forward, made Lucy impotent.

"Do I have to put a sign on everything, or a lock? Don't you know that decent people don't pry and snoop into other people's business?"

"Tell me what the scrapbook's all about," Helen answered. She seemed impervious to Lucy's anger and scorn, impelled by a curiosity about the odd collection of clippings she had puzzled through. "I want you to tell me what it's all about," she insisted with a pitiful stubbornness.

"It's all about things you'd never understand," Lucy answered. "Like decency and honor; it's about fine people doing good things; it's about people who aren't looking out for themselves. You didn't see anything there about somebody sneaking into somebody else's private affairs, did you?"

Helen stayed on the floor where Lucy had found her. She had not changed her position; only the slow movement of her thumb, as it unconsciously caressed the clump of holy cards in her hand, indicated that she was thinking of anything.

"You didn't know any of those people in these newspaper stories, did you?" she asked in the same mild, puzzled voice.

"I *recognize* them," Lucy answered with scorn, drawn into the conversation in spite of herself.

"And the pictures . . . do you recognize them, too?" Helen asked.

"Look, it's none of your business. Now get out of my stuff, and I don't want to catch you in my things again," Lucy said, working up her anger at Helen again. "If you want to look through a scrapbook, make one of your own."

"I wouldn't know what to put in it," Helen said tiredly, and then she began to laugh, a terrible, rasping sound that struck Lucy as old, dry, and dusty.

"The only scrapbook I ever started was of movie stars, but I got tired of that; it didn't mean anything after a while. Yours is all just plain people, and all of them men," she said wonderingly. "Some of these jokers are almost ugly—*nice,* but you've got to admit this guy's no prize for looks . . ." She put down the stack of holy cards and began turning the pages of the scrapbook backward until she came to the face of a man in his middle-forties, slightly balding, the mouth serious and kind, the eyes intelligent under the dark brows.

"You know, he reminds me of somebody—I can't even remember who, but I'm sure I've seen this guy *somewhere* before . . ."

Lucy bent down and snapped the cover shut. "Here," she said, handing the book to Helen. "If you like it so much, keep it."

"But it's yours," Helen began.

"It's yours if you like it so much," Lucy said.

"Gee, Lucy," Helen said.

"Don't say I never gave you anything," Lucy answered. She began replacing things in her dresser drawer. "And if you don't mind, I'd appreciate it if you didn't go crawling through my things like some sneaky cockroach."

She felt unreasonably angry at Helen's having her scrapbook; her generous impulse had been surprised out of her, taken by force rather than freely given.

"Look, if you don't want me to have this . . ."

"Take it, take it," Lucy insisted peevishly. "In fact, take my bath while you're at it; I won't have time for that, either." She walked away from Helen, went to the bathroom and turned off the tub faucets, then washed her face and hands in the sink.

"I wish *everything* I tried didn't always end up half baked," she mumbled to herself. She checked the clock and saw that she was five minutes late for her appointment downstairs. She hurried a comb through her hair, put on a clean dress, and left Helen stretched across her bed studying the anonymous faces of men.

She could hear the low murmur of voices in the Bishop's Parlor on the first floor and knew it was Sister Christine and Miss Fairfax. For just a moment she was tempted to hang back and listen unobserved. It struck her as something Helen would do and she cleared her throat noisily and walked in.

"Good afternoon, Sister. Hello, Miss Fairfax." Her eyes darted nervously around the room for information. Sunlight slanted through the high windows, showing a dazzle of dust motes in the air. Marcella wasn't there; it must not be a family problem. She offered them a guarded smile.

"Sister tells me you sprained your ankle. How is it?"

Lucy looked at her ankle, moved her foot indifferently. "Oh, that," she said. "It's fine."

"Sit down, Lucy," Sister said.

Lucy sat down. She ran her finger over the carved arm of the chair she had taken. The dark wood curved into the shapes of snakes that twisted their way around the arms and down to the legs of the chair, where each wooden serpent caught a tail in his half-opened mouth. Lucy had studied that chair dozens of times, always meaning to discover whether the snakes were devouring themselves or one another. She had never been able to unsort their intricacies.

"Sister tells me she's spoken to you about the possibility of going to a foster home," Miss Fairfax said.

"So that's it," Lucy thought to herself. Her eyes dropped away from the snakes and looked directly at Miss Fairfax.

"Don't you have anything to say that Sister doesn't tell you?" she asked.

In the void of silence that Lucy's remark created, Miss Fairfax rearranged the half-dozen fine silver bracelets that circled her wrist. Her nails were long and well cared for. A large, square-cut engagement diamond on her left hand sent splinters of light onto the walls each time she moved her finger.

Lucy remembered the day Miss Fairfax had come for her monthly visit to St. Michael's wearing the ring, blushing at their exclamations of surprise and pleasure. She had seemed jewel-like herself that day, so golden, so small and exquisitely wrought, the shy happiness in her gray eyes shared with each of them like a promise.

"Can we come to your wedding?" Lucy had asked her then, and when Miss Fairfax took Lucy's hand in her own and said, "Of course you can," Lucy had loved her. The same sense of ripened joy, the air of a fragile and untouchable happiness that had clung to Miss Fairfax like a blessing and made Lucy love her then, was intolerable now. Miss Fairfax was like the rest of them. The ring on her finger was a sign of her ultimate indifference. It sealed off her own life from Lucy's; it was the signal of how little they had to do with one another. Any suggestion that there was something Lucy might take, borrow even, from Miss Fairfax's existence was a lie, a sham. Lucy was not going to be tricked.

"Well?" she asked moodily, returning to her unanswered question, enjoying the uncomfortable silence that exaggerated the sound of the silver bracelets chattering against one another. Sister Christine said nothing, presiding with seemingly detached interest over the encounter. Lucy felt the familiar sense of helplessness. She was always cornered by Sister Christine. She returned her attention to Miss Fairfax.

"Why don't you tell me what you're here for, instead of telling me what Sister has told you about me?" she said.

Miss Fairfax looked up from her wrist. She locked the fingers of her two hands together and held them an inch or so above her lap. Then she shrugged. "It's all part of the same thing, Lucy," she said. "You know that." Her eyes begged to be understood. Lucy looked away from her eyes. She was not ready for the compromise which that soft, pleading look might force her into. Her glance refused that face that begged and accused so gently. She studied, instead, Miss Fairfax's throat. The skin there was soft and white as a child's. Where the notched collar of a green linen shirtwaist dress lay back against the narrow shelf of collarbone, Lucy could see, or thought she could see, the same shade of glassy green repeated in the lacy edging and delicate strap of a slip. She looked down to the hem of the dress where it formed a straight ledge over the crossed knees. The same lacy green, an extravagant surge of it, broke softly under the hedge of crisp linen. Conscious that she was about to say something gauche, Lucy looked Miss Fairfax full in the face.

"Does your underwear always match what you're wearing?" she said.

Miss Fairfax colored, fluttered her fingers at her throat for an instant until they caught hold of a fine chain that supported a single pearl pendant. She moved the pearl back and forth slightly, let it drop into the thumb-sized well at the base of her throat, and then, as though that settled something, she smiled.

"Not always," she said. "Do you always ask questions that have nothing to do with the case?"

Lucy saw that she had lost control. She was not unhappy about it. It occurred to her that her habit of embarrassing people was slightly tiresome, a childish habit, really, that she exercised to gain attention.

"I don't want to go to a foster home," she said.

"Why is that?" Miss Fairfax asked.

"I'm not looking for a fake family," Lucy said.

"What are you looking for?" Miss Fairfax said.

"I don't know; I really don't know. How *could* I know?" she added after a moment.

Miss Fairfax said nothing. Three, four times she clicked the nail of her ring finger under the pale enameled thumbnail. The tiny sound took up the entire room. Miss Fairfax suddenly realized the sound they all sat listening to was of her own making. She stopped and let her hands lie still on her lap.

"Lucy, something unusual has turned up. It's quite out of the ordinary, really." Miss Fairfax glanced briefly toward Sister Christine, as though asking for confirmation. Sister Christine shuttered her eyes, nodded her head forward in a single, slow affirmative movement.

"Usually," Miss Fairfax continued, encouraged by that single movement of the head, "our foster families contact the agency. We investigate them and then try to find a child that we think will be best suited to that particular placement."

Lucy nodded wearily, wondering if Miss Fairfax, or Sister Christine for that matter, could possibly imagine how hideous it was to sit listening to talk about agencies, placements, investigations, knowing that no matter how they disguised the language, they were talking about some sort of a commodity, and that commodity was you. She knew exactly what was about to be said. They had discovered the perfect slot, the not-to-be-believed square hole for the square peg that was Lucy Brannan. And now they wanted to screw her into it and see what would happen.

"It's hardly a case of 'virtue rewarded' if I do say so myself," Miss Fairfax said. She was smiling fondly, indulgently, and her tone of voice was that of a parent who feels compelled to offer a gentle scolding to a child who has accomplished something marvelous by disregarding a long-standing family rule.

Lucy was puzzled into attention. Miss Fairfax sensed the shift in attitude and hastened on.

"We've been contacted by a family who asked particularly about *you*." Miss Fairfax bent forward on her chair toward Lucy. "They're not asking for a *foster* child, Lucy; they're asking for *you*."

"Who are they?" Lucy asked suspiciously.

"Their name is Wyatt: Mr. and Mrs. Wyatt . . ."

"I don't know them," Lucy said flatly. She had thought to recognize the name, to solve, without further complication, the mystery of being wanted that had so excited Miss Fairfax.

"You don't know them, but they've seen you." Miss Fairfax was obviously enjoying the suspense.

Sister Christine's hands flicked impatiently on her lap.

"Mr. Wyatt saw you when you made your television debut," she said dryly.

Lucy blushed, went pale, then blushed again, remembering her remark to the camera that had devoured Marcella's strange observations the day of the picnic. Lucy had not appeared on the film when it was shown on the evening news report the following day, and she had never mentioned the incident to Sister Christine.

"Apparently you impressed Mr. Wyatt," Sister Christine said, taking over the conversation from Miss Fairfax. "Mr. Wyatt is a film producer and he didn't want you lost on the cutting-room floor."

Lucy could not tell if Sister Christine was smiling or not. She did not dare, just then, to look at her face. Her heart felt, for the moment, as though it had an existence all its own, shivering wildly against her ribs.

"Mr. Wyatt thought enough about you to ask Mrs. Wyatt to come down to the station and see for herself." Sister Christine looked over to Miss Fairfax, who sat, chastened and still in her chair, apparently sensing that Sister Christine had taken over her job for her.

"It *is* unusual," Sister Christine said, by way of reconciling her cool approach to Miss Fairfax's eager enthusiasm.

"Miss Fairfax has been to see them several times. They're anxious to come to St. Michael's to meet you." Sister Christine sat back and spread her hands, palms downward on her knees. Lucy watched the unfamiliar gesture with fascination; Sister seemed to be counting her fingers.

"But they know nothing about me," Lucy said wonderingly. "Oh, I know you've told them everything," she said, looking over to Miss Fairfax, "but they really don't know what I'm like at all."

"I agree," Sister Christine said. "It's quite an act of faith on their part." She lifted her eyes to look at Lucy directly.

"And they do know a little," Miss Fairfax said, coming back into the conversation with a tentative smile, speaking, Lucy thought, almost timidly. "They're next-door neighbors to Dr. Pelligrini."

A surprise, a shock of joy went through Lucy. Twice she drew in her breath to speak and twice found her head shaking wordlessly.

"I can't believe it," she finally said, believing it more than anything. It was true; she realized that it was so, sensed the mysterious certainty of it. Its very incredibility lent it an authority that no reasonable explanation could ever have.

She felt as though an inner skin were cracking open; layer upon layer of it seemed to split, peel back, curl dry upon itself. She could almost hear the sound of it. And then she realized it was the sound of her own breath coming in sharp, shallow darts. She did not know how long she sat there, waiting for the feeling to go away, knowing that the two people who sat watching her could not see what she could feel, and yet they watched her. She felt raw and exposed, yet fascinated by the tender and untouched creature who lay, naked and new, in her place.

No harm must come to that newborn presence, so frail and so fresh, she resolved. She would guard it with her life, give it nothing but good things to grow on. The chance was hers, the choice of each action that would nourish it to life was her own responsibility. Nothing must go wrong this time—nothing. She considered her words and spoke them with slow care.

"I want the Wyatts to come," she said. "I want them to come and meet me."

# Chapter 10

Lucy sat very still. It was the best way to quiet the shivering of her hands while she waited. Her hands were the only visible part of herself that she had not brought under control for the meeting this afternoon. She had discovered that the nervous swinging of her foot simply could not take over if she uncrossed her legs and planted both feet on the floor. She had taught her eyes to stay clear of the sudden tears that would swarm there each time she thought of what was about to happen; if she fixed on any inanimate object and forced her mind to study its size, shape, colors, points of contact with other objects, then the tears would pull back to their secret hiding place, leaving her eyes with a burned-out feeling that was gritty, but dry as sand. She had not touched a soft drink or a candy bar for the two weeks since Miss Fairfax had told her about the Wyatts. The skin of her face was almost entirely clear. She had brushed her hair with not one but close to three or four hundred strokes each day, sometimes until the skin of her scalp felt sore and burdened by its fine black handful of hair.

Sister Christine had given her a new dress, small blue-and-white checks with a tucked shirtwaist front trimmed in tiny bands of white lace that made a secret of her small breasts. She had wanted brand-new underwear, too. Sister Christine told her she had more than enough as it was. Lucy had taken seven dollars of her own money. It had taken her forever to save that from the rare occasions when Mamma would stuff a dirty wrinkled dollar into her coat pocket as she left from a visit. She had gone to the five-and-ten-cent store and bought a stiff new bra, a pair of plain white nylon panties, and a half slip trimmed in cheap cotton lace that would ravel to shreds the first time she washed it. She knew that when she bought it, but she didn't mind. She didn't intend to wash it until after it had served its purpose this afternoon. And the feeling of newness from the skin out was worth every penny. Nothing had ever happened to her in a single stitch she had on. Except for the sandals. But she was wearing them again on purpose. They had brought her luck before. She buckled them on gladly, remembering in a rush that day that had been, all unknown to her, the secret beginning of this day.

She *would* see Dr. Pelligrini again; she had known all along, somewhere deep inside her she had known that he would be a friend to her. She had known it reading the Lucy poems she had asked Sister Justin to get for her. And she had feasted on the secret of that book, letting Sister Justin believe that *she* was responsible for Lucy's interest in the English Romantic poets. She had learned certain parts of the Lucy poems by heart, and she would whisper them softly to herself in the bathroom when the water was running, or out in back of the house, checking over her shoulder to make sure that no one was creeping up behind her. " 'No mate, no comrade Lucy knew;/She dwelt on a wide moor,/ —The sweetest thing that ever grew/ Beside a human door!' " He had known that was there before he had told her she was in the poems. And there were other stanzas that had her name on them too, she had discovered, even when the word *Lucy* wasn't there in print. " 'Tonight will be a stormy night—/ You to the town must go;/ And take a lantern, Child, to light/ Your mother through the snow.' " That one made her throat tighten each time she read it. She had never told him about Mamma, but she was certain he knew it all without her telling. He surely knew everything about her. It had to be so. " 'The storm came on before its time:/ She wandered up and down;/ And many a hill did Lucy climb:/ But never reached the town.' "

Her eyes were beginning to blur. She fastened them on the skirt of her dress. She saw how the shape of her knees determined the folds of the material. She searched among the small checks, finally discovered, on a blue one, the minute flick of the white hemming stitch. She followed the path of the hemstitch, first on blue, then barely discernible on white checks, until her eyes were clear and dry. It was working, she was learning; if she could hold onto that and keep going, she might even be able to teach her mind and heart to be still and obedient to her will.

She waited alone, soothed by the dull droning sound of the large fan that stood at the end of the dormitory by the door of Sister Justin's cubicle. The other four had left after lunch with free tickets for a downtown movie. Lucy had let them believe she was being punished for something, said, with an honest edge to her voice, "I won't be going with you, thanks to Sister Christine." They all knew she had been called down to Sister's office that morning, and a murmur of sympathy briefly interrupted their noon-meal chatter about the afternoon they had planned.

"What's she got against you, anyway?" Joanne had asked with narrowed eyes. "Every time I turn around, she's got you by the collar."

"That woman is a witch," Helen said.

"Witch spelled with a capital B," Ginny said.

Only Carol remained silent, meeting Lucy's eyes briefly, encountering there another splinter of secretiveness, like so many others that had been closing them off from one another lately. Lucy had refused the question in Carol's eyes, and without Lucy to draw on, Carol had discovered she had nothing to say. Lucy saw what was happening; she felt brushes of discomfort each time Carol bid for a return to the old closeness. Abruptly, adroitly, by turns, she fended off the confidences that came her way, she found reasons not to go anywhere alone with Carol, she slept, or pretended to sleep on the hot summer nights that had always been full of whispered conversations between their two beds, which were next to one another. And she had told Carol nothing, absolutely nothing, about the Wyatts. In fact, she had told no one, not Mamma, not even Marcella. They would have to know soon, but there could be no telling until Lucy was sure herself. After today she would know whether there was anything to tell. She was glad that Sister Christine and Sister Justin had arranged for the meeting on a day when the others would not be there to buzz around like vultures, feasting on someone else's flesh.

The moment she thought out Sister Justin's name, the door to the cubicle opened as though there had been some mysterious connection between Lucy's mind and Sister Justin's presence. It did not even strike Lucy as strange.

"Two o'clock, Lucy," Sister Justin said. The steel of her voice was suddenly full of gravel. She cleared her throat of the intrusion, touching her fingers delicately to her lips. Outside, beneath the window, there was the sound of a car driving up, stopping; first one, then a second car door slammed shut, and a few seconds later the front-door bell sounded its alarm all the way up to the third floor. "It's time for you"—the gravel was there again. Sister Justin cleared it away once more, shaking her small head impatiently. "Time for you to go," she finished, breaking into a sudden fit of coughing but managing, in the midst of it, to wave one thin hand toward the door while the other hand reached for a handkerchief and muffled her mouth against any further words she might have wanted to say to Lucy.

Lucy got up from the small straight-backed chair where she had been sitting. Her hands smoothed out the skirt of her dress carefully, then reached up on either side of her head to puff out the thin black hair that had already started to separate over her ears. Then, with nothing more to do, the hand dropped awkwardly to her sides, felt vainly for pockets that were not there, finally met one another in a childish clasp above her stomach.

"I guess I'll go down, then," she said lamely, surprised

at the high thin sound of her own voice that went unanswered.

Her fingers were moist and she trailed them over the banister all the way downstairs. There was a feathery, interior tickling that began just beneath her throat and spread downward to where her legs branched off from the rest of her body. The feeling settled in her knees, where it turned to a terrible trembling. Sister Christine's office was off to the right, far down the front corridor. She followed the floorboards, counted what nails she could find and saw that she stood in the doorway. "Here's Lucy now," Sister Christine said, standing up from behind her desk, interrupting whatever it was she had been saying. She came forward, taking Lucy's hand and leading her like a small child up to the man and woman who sat on tan leather chairs, two of three drawn up in a semicircle by the side of the desk. The man, sandy-haired and warm-looking, stood up with nervous, friendly impatience. He put out his hand to be shaken. She clasped it with her own and said, "Hello, Mr. Wyatt," trying to control the fatuous grin that began to overtake her face as she recognized the man who had not wanted to photograph the banner on the bus the day of the picnic.

"And Eloise . . ." He dropped Lucy's hand, after patting it twice, and chopped at the air in the direction of his wife.

"Mrs. Wyatt," Sister Christine said firmly, and drew Lucy toward the woman.

"Maybe it will be easiest just to call me Mother," she said, but she laughed as she said it, not insisting on anything, easily and gracefully, as she undid her long legs from their crossed posture, bent forward, seemed ready to stand but did not stand, only leaned forward to Lucy, who could not stop breathing the quiet dazzle of perfume that lay about the room because this woman was there. "Hello, Lucy," she said then, and did not stop smiling but sat back and touched the empty chair beside her.

Lucy had never seen anyone so beautiful. Her dark eyes bloomed like twin flowers or stars, and though her eyes were dark and rich, the rest of her face was fair and fresh; the cheekbones rising high and smooth under those remarkable eyes, the lips, slightly rouged with pink, soft and composed, but with a sense of readiness about them parted to show fine small teeth as though waiting each moment to smile, to speak, to take a message from the eyes. Her hair was the color of ripe wheat and it was drawn back and upward from the brow and the nape of the neck, bound into thick twisted coils of heavy gold at the back of her head. But all around the hairline tiny tendrils broke free of the smooth shining crown and curled with a will of their own, catching at the sun to form a nimbus of light. Her nose and her neck seemed to belong to one another in a way that other people's did not. Both were long and fine with a partrician elegance about them, and yet her nose fluted slightly upward when she smiled, almost crinkled, lending it an air of merriment, and her neck had a habit of twisting slightly to left or to right to support the changing angle of her head, which she tilted slightly toward the person who spoke to her. It was an engaging mannerism which flattered speaker and listener at the same time.

Lucy found herself studying the motions of the head at it cocked to one side when Lucy said "Hello," dropped slightly backward, chin raised expectantly toward Sister

Christine, who spoke next, saying, "I've never seen Lucy so shy since the day I met her," then dropped forward, the chin ducked down as she broke into a generous smile; the eyes widened and deepened for all of them in the room.

"I think we all feel a little shy at the moment," she said. "At least, *I* do." And then everyone was able to laugh. "But I don't think that's going to last very long," she said at precisely the right moment in their laughter, not allowing it to go on too long, not letting it dwindle off into an awkward silence. "Lucy"—now she was doing that trick again with her head, bringing it around, inclining it swiftly toward Lucy—"I'm sure there are things you'd like to ask us. We've had an unfair advantage—Sister Christine and Sarah Fairfax have told us so much about you—what would you like to know about us?" She made a gift of the question, handed it to Lucy and sat back with eager anticipation lighting her face.

"I just want to know if you really want me to live with you," Lucy said painfully, aware of the bald gracelessness of her question, but unable to be anything but direct.

"We wouldn't be here if we didn't," Mr. Wyatt said, sliding into the conversation, striking out his words crisply, quickly, with an air of cheerful reasonability. He smiled puckishly, his face brightened with sudden color, stopping a shade short of a blush, and he threw a glance at each of them—Sister Christine, Lucy, his wife—as if to ask them all if that wasn't perfectly clear.

"But why?" Lucy asked next, needing to get it all over with at once, before something happened to snatch away the answer she hungered after. She had asked the question of him, but she turned instinctively to Mrs. Wyatt, as toward light, for the answer.

For an instant something trembled beneath the surface. The lips drew up into a round O, faltered, dropped, and were held back from any expression by the small white teeth that settled momentarily, restrainingly, on the rosy lower lip. The eyes, too, deepened and brooded, threw on a shield against something painful. Then her eyes cleared, lay wide and open, quickened with something deeper than whatever had troubled, so briefly, their calm surface.

"Because we love you," she said with terrible, grave simplicity. "And because Tom and I believe in love at first sight—and second sight."

Now she made mischief with her smile, turning it first on her husband, flirtatious, teasing him until he put back his head and laughed out loud, blushing completely this time, but seeming glad to be doing so for her sake.

"That's a private joke, Sister," he said, speaking to Sister Christine, but apologizing to Lucy in case she had felt shut out by their secret.

"I'm sure you have lots of them," Sister Christine said. She spoke with neither approval nor censure apparent in her voice. Lucy quaked at the thought that Sister Christine might say something that would make them change their mind about having her join their family.

"Do you have any other—I mean, do you have any children?" Lucy asked.

"None but you—if you'll have us." She smiled so directly, Lucy felt her heart stumble for a moment. "Is your house big enough—I mean . . ."

"Oh, it's quite big enough; in fact, you might find it too big," Mr. Wyatt said.

"Oh, no," Lucy interrupted quickly, defending herself against the possibility of saying anything wrong.

"Well, don't be sure until you've seen it," he said. "Eloise and I often think it's foolish to keep such a large house for just the two of us."

"You know I have a sister; I'm sure you know that," Lucy said. She laughed nervously.

"Yes . . ."

"Lucy—" Sister Christine's head moved in a single negative gesture, so slight, so slow that it could have been mistaken as a mere turning toward Lucy by anyone who did not know her well. "Lucy, Marcella isn't ready for a foster home."

"Oh, I didn't mean that." She bent toward Mrs. Wyatt, then jerked her head around to include Mr. Wyatt. "You know I didn't mean you should take Marcella too. I only meant, I only wondered if you knew . . ."

"It's all right, darling, we know," Mrs. Wyatt said. Lucy had never heard anyone use the word "darling" except in a movie. Mrs. Wyatt used it so easily, so sweetly. The grace of it ravished Lucy. She tried to smile and found she could only stare.

"We hope Sister Christine will let Marcella come to visit you at home just as soon as we're all settled," she said quietly. "We hope she can come often."

Lucy had stopped listening. She meant to listen, but the words "at home" stuck in her ears, clogged the sound of whatever else was being said. They were all saying something; it seemed as though they were all talking at once. Mr. Wyatt was rubbing the back of his neck with the back of his hand and smiling as he said whatever it was he said. Sister Christine was nodding to him, including Lucy somehow in her affirmation, but holding something back still; giving, but not surrendering Lucy to him. Lucy saw it in the cautionary, still-to-be-proved aspect of her glance, the slight, guarded angle of declination with which she bowed her head slightly forward to the Wyatts while her hands toyed with the cap of her fountain pen, which lay unsheathed on the desk. Mrs. Wyatt's hands closed over her purse. She spoke, and sound returned to Lucy's ears as she heard Mrs. Wyatt saying, "Then, may we come for Lucy on Saturday?"

Lucy nodded her head to Sister Christine as though cueing her to the proper answer.

"Will that be too soon, Lucy?" Sister asked.

It took Lucy a second to switch the shaking of her head from yes to urgent no. Then she found her voice. "I could be ready in five minutes," she said.

The Wyatts smiled indulgently. Sister Christine did not join them.

"I think five days will be a little more sensible," she said. "You'll have some packing to do. I wouldn't want you to forget anything."

"I want to forget *everything*," Lucy said. She spoke passionately, sounding like herself for the first time that afternoon, the foreign thinness gone from her voice. She turned away from the stubborn, suffering look that clouded Sister Christine's eyes. She offered her face, instead, to Mrs. Wyatt, whose tender, troubled glance assured her that she understood how Lucy felt. Mr. Wyatt was patting at his forehead and upper lip with a folded handkerchief. Lucy could see that he was eager to leave, now that everything was settled. She stood up, plucked discreetly at the skirt of the dress that was clinging all the way through the slip to the moist backs of her thighs.

"I'll be ready on Saturday," she said to both of them.

"Good," they answered in unison, then turned to smile at one another at the felicity of having said exactly the same thing at the same time.

"May I be excused now, Sister?" Lucy asked archly, turning to Sister Christine, mincing her words a little, mocking the formality of the phrase by the tone of her voice.

"Yes, Lucy. You are excused." Sister Christine managed to make the words sound as though they meant a great deal. She had a way of doing that; it had always unnerved Lucy. It was an entire frame of mind that she was glad to be getting away from. She backed out of the office, feeling taken down somehow, hovered in the doorway for an instant wanting to secure everything for herself, but only managed to smile and wave clumsily at the three people who sat waiting for her to leave. "Well, goodbye then," she said, and left abruptly, not quite clearing the doorframe, striking her elbow against the indifferent dark wood that sent a shattering nervous chase up the entire length of her arm. None of them had noticed, and she hurried down the corridor massaging her elbow vigorously, shaking her head and saying softly, under her breath, "God, how I hate this house."

# Chapter 11

Lucy had been over it all in her mind a dozen times, but now that she was actually on her way to see Mamma, to meet her face to face with the fact of the new home, all the sensible words and right reasons slipped around in her brain, making a clutter of the order she had so carefully constructed.

"It's not as though Mamma doesn't already know," she told herself for the third time in five minutes. She had walked around the block twice after getting off the bus, waiting until she felt able to open the front door and see her mother. She had talked to her about it on the phone; she knew Miss Fairfax had been here to see her mother already. But none of that was the same thing. This would be the real encounter with Mamma, Lucy knew that.

She knew, too, that people were watching her. The old lady who sat in the upstairs bedroom window across the street, leaning her elbows on a windowsill that bloomed profusely with red geraniums potted in Crisco cans, that old lady had waved at her, though Lucy pretended not to see it. It had rained while Lucy was on the bus, but now the sun shone down fiercely, making steamy patterns of vaporized heat on the sidewalks that were already drying. Children, some in dirty clothing, some dressed in nothing but grayish underpants, lined the curb, sailing leaves, bits of paper, scraps of twig down the gutter that still swirled with the recent rain. They looked up from their game curiously at her. She was a stranger to all of them. She tried to smile.

"Hello," she said.

"Ricky's got a boat," a tiny girl announced, and turned back to the curb. Lucy stopped, lingered with them for a moment. "I used to live here too, you know," she wanted to say. But she said nothing. They would not understand what it was she would be trying to say about belonging here. Instead, she stepped closer to them, bent to inspect the makeshift boat that reeled crazily in the eddies of muddy water.

"Hey, lady, you're stepping on our rainbow," a little boy cried out. His voice was curiously hoarse and adult for his size. Lucy looked at him in confusion.

"Move, lady, move," he urged angrily, and the rest of them took up the cry, shrieking at Lucy to move, jumping up and down in a sudden frenzy, a confusion of thin, dirty, dwarf-like arms and legs that flailed the air about them, insisting that she was stepping on their rainbow. Lucy looked about wonderingly. There was sunlight and water, but there was no rainbow. Her head quivered on her neck in a series of small puzzled darting motions. Her hand moved slowly about her, interrogating the air for the whereabouts of the rainbow.

"Hey, look at her, she's crazy too, just like her old lady," the child with the deep voice croaked, and laughter broke about her ears in a shower of sound.

"Your mother's waitin' for ya," another child said, flinging the words at her over his shoulder as he crouched, leapt high into the air, and dropped down squarely into the small river of rain, setting up a miniature explosion of dirty water. He stooped there in the gutter for a moment, then stood up, regarding with mock horror the streams of dirty water that coursed down the insides of his legs.

"Oh, look what I done, right here in the street too," he announced. "And look, I done it right on the lady's dress," he said, pointing to Lucy's blue-and-white-checked dress, which was speckled with the splashes of rain that his antics had flung up from the gutter. The crowd of children scattered like a flock of birds, dancing up and down on the sidewalk, hopping about in the street, chattering in a shrill cacophony of delight. Lucy stepped back from them instinctively. She looked down to inspect the soiled skirt of her dress and saw, in the spot where she had been standing, the shimmer of an old oil spot that glistened with iridescent color. Freshened by the recent rain, blues, golds, mauves, and greens shimmered in random blots of color at her feet.

"Ah," she thought to herself, "so that's their rainbow." She plucked at her soggy skirt, tried smoothing it out with her fingers. It was no use. And she had wanted to look just right for Mamma today. She had wanted to look exactly as she had looked the day she met the Wyatts.

"That'll be dry soon," the tiny girl said wisely, watching Lucy's face.

"It's all right," Lucy said.

"The ice-cream man comes in a minute," the child said. "We don't have any money."

"Neither do I," Lucy said.

"What's in your purse?" she asked craftily.

"Only my carfare to get back home," Lucy said.

"Where do you live?"

"Far from here," Lucy said.

"What's that big lump in your purse?" the child asked.

"It's something I brought for my mother," Lucy said.

"Sometimes your mother gives us money," she said.

Lucy felt a twitch of amazement at the fact that they all seemed to know that she belonged to Mamma. The information did not embarrass them as it did her. They stood around her, curious and unashamed.

"Do you have *anything* for us?" one finally asked.

"Nothing," Lucy said, shaking her head sadly. Still they did not leave. They stood there regarding her solemnly.

"Well, are you coming to see me, or are you holding court on the sidewalk?" Mamma's voice, querulous and amused, called from the screen door.

"I'm coming, Mamma," Lucy said, turning instantly to the summons.

"Oh, look how she's dressed up today," the deep voice said. A boy whistled an imitation of male appreciation, and the flock of children broke loose again, filling the street with shouts and laughter.

Lucy hurried in and closed the door against the sound of their voices. Mamma was outrageous, Lucy thought. She had dressed up like this just to torment her. She was wearing a thin voile dress, white, with huge, horrible black flowers that climbed over her breasts and hips. She was not wearing a slip. Clad in loose-fitting, mid-thigh rayon trunks that sheltered only half the outline of her pitiful thin legs, and a cotton-knit undershirt with narrow straps that could not support the dejection of her breasts, the shape of her body was visible to Lucy. Mamma was wearing white silk shoes with thick square heels, and nylon stockings that wrinkled around her ankles. Her head was elegantly wrapped in a white silk turban. Slung around her throat, knotted loosely into a noose effect, hanging down far beyond the cameo brooch that fastened the neck of her dress just below the collarbone, were the pearls, the real pearls that were Mamma's now, and had been Mamma's mother's, and would be Lucy's some day.

Mamma was studying Lucy with a shrewd look. "I've dressed for the occasion," she said innocently. "I didn't want you to remember me as someone who never managed to get out of a bathrobe."

"Mamma, you talk as though I'm never going to see you again." Lucy spoke with irritation to cover the anguish she felt.

"Maybe you won't." She cut short Lucy's protest. "Maybe you won't want to," she said with malicious amusement. "Oh, I wouldn't blame you. Don't, as a matter of fact. Let's see . . . not counting phone calls, it was February and cold the last time you managed to get down to the slums; now it's July and warm." She sighed and shrugged her shoulders with an air of injured fatalism.

"Mamma, I was sick in March—everybody had hideous colds—and I was so busy in April . . ."

"Sick in March, busy in April, merry in May, joyous in July." Mamma made a nursery chant of it, jogging her head from side to side to mark the rhythm of what she was saying. Lucy stared at the incongruous turban with fascination.

"Honey, are they good people?" Mamma asked suddenly, giving up the game, dropping onto the red sofa and bending slightly toward Lucy, who had taken the chair by the window. Lucy saw that Mamma had clutched her left wrist with her right hand where it lay in her lap but that it still trembled slightly and would not be still.

"I know their name is Wyatt, I know they're rich, I know they're cultivated, I know they're childless, I know they're interested in you"—she shot this out like a litany that needed to be gotten through. She smiled at Lucy like a precocious child.

"You see how well I learn my lessons?" she asked brightly. "I've been schooled by Miss Fairfax, your lovely lady, your . . . one, two, three, four, five . . . my stars, this is going to be your fifth."

"Mamma, what are you counting off?"

"Why, your mothers, honey. I declare, you're going to be the *most* reared, if not the best-reared, young lady in town. You have Sister Christine, Sister Justin, Miss Fairfax, Mrs. Wyatt, and then there's me."

"There's you, Mamma," Lucy said. "There's really only you."

"Do you know that, honey? Do you really know that?" Her mother jumped up and began pacing the small room anxiously. "Lord knows, I've wanted to do my best by you.

Why, I'd cut off my arm if I thought it would do you any good." She began rubbing her arm absently as though feeling pain there.

"Mamma, sit down, you're making me nervous."

"Honey, I'm not making you anything. You're *made*. And I'm the one who did it. Why, I gave my body and blood to make you. You're my *child*." Her voice had begun to rise, but it softened into a moan on the last word.

"Look, Mamma, if you want me to walk out right this minute, you just start crying. Now, I'm not going to sit here and watch you cry. I mean it."

She began to get up from the chair, as though to leave.

"You just sit right back, honey, because I'm not going to cry. Why, I never meant to cry at all. I've got lemonade for you," she said, and stood up, fussing with the pearls at her throat for a minute. "And you're not to budge, you hear. I've got it all set out and I'll get it myself."

Lucy sat back, relieved. The first part of it was over, and Mamma had done it for her. All the time she had spent constructing ways to tell Mamma to her face, that time was all dissolved by the fact of Mamma's being the first to say it, the first to name the Wyatts. Now it was Lucy's turn to tell her what they were like. The refrigerator door closed, the sound of things being set out on a cheap tin tray and the glassy chattering of ice cubes announced Mamma's return.

There was a heavy pitcher full of lemonade and two empty glasses on the tray. Mamma set it down on the wide windowsill. The lemonade was home-made, not the kind out of a can or a bottle of concentrate. The liquid swam with tiny fragments of fruit. Mamma picked up the pitcher, supported the bottom of it with one hand while she swirled it to stir up the sediment of sugar and pulp that had settled to the bottom.

"The best part, the real heart of the matter, is always at the bottom of things," she intoned solemnly, swirling, staring, brooding like a priestess over an offering.

"Hey, Mamma, how about some lemonade," Lucy reminded her gently.

"Patience, patience," Mamma said. "Never be impatient for your pleasures. They come faster, they last longer if you don't go grabbing after them. There now." She filled the two glasses.

"You're having lemonade with me," Lucy said.

"I vary my intake from time to time," Mamma said.

Lucy drank thirstily, emptying more than half the glass. "That's good," she said.

"It gets better as you go along," Mamma said, and broke into a fit of laughing. "Oh, Lucy, you're such a solemn child. You always were. Don't you ever loosen the latches?" She sipped at her drink.

"What do you mean?" Lucy asked defensively.

"Let down. Undo. Spin out. Why, you don't even know what it feels like to let go, do you, honey?" Mamma's eyes took on a faraway look.

"When you were just a little girl, you clutched at everything, wore the hair right off your doll babies holding onto them in your sleep. You broke every pair of shoelaces you ever had because you pulled on them so tight to make sure your shoes weren't going anywhere but where your two little feet took them. Why, I remember once when I got you and your sister gas balloons; it wouldn't do for you to hold onto yours—you made me tie it to your wrist and you were a big eight-year-old child at the time. Marcella, she let go of hers right off. She wasn't yet three years old and I thought it had slipped out of her hand. 'Mamma will get you another, baby,' I said to her, thinking she was going to cry. I got her another and she couldn't wait to get her hands on it just to let it loose. And then that baby turned her little face up to me, her eyes as big as saucers, and she said to me, 'Look what goes, Mamma, look what goes.' "

"What did I do with mine?" Lucy asked.

Mamma smiled and leaned forward, laying her hand on Lucy's lap and shaking her head sadly.

"Honey, you took yours home, untied it from your wrist only to tie it onto the chair by your bed. I wanted you to at least let it ride up to the ceiling, but you wouldn't have it that way. And in the morning, when you woke up, all the helium was out of it—it was nothing but a withered-up piece of red rubber tied fast to the chair by a skinny old string."

Lucy had finished her lemonade while Mamma talked. She stared down into the empty glass, feeling profoundly sad.

"I guess I'll have more," she said.

"Why don't you wait a bit; I'm only half through mine," Mamma said.

"There's an awful lot of lemonade there, Mamma. I don't plan to drink you dry," Lucy said, reaching for the pitcher to refill her own glass. The weight of the pitcher surprised her wrist. She found she could hardly control it. She set the pitcher down for a moment, methodically clamped the glass between her knees, and returned to the pitcher, using both hands as Mamma had done. She found herself concentrating on the task of pouring a glass of lemonade. It seemed terribly important to do it properly.

She watched the liquid break over the beak of the pitcher, studied the shreds of fruit as they hurried over the edge, urged on by the cubes of ice that rushed forward when she tilted the pitcher.

"There's something to it," she heard herself thinking. "There's something to everything if you just look close enough."

"Mamma," she chose each word carefully, singling out the sounds as she spoke them, "I never knew it before, but pouring lemonade is beautiful."

She had said that out loud, not spoken it in her mind. She knew, because it sounded entirely different inside your head when you said something, instead of just thinking it.

"Lucy, for pity's sake, you're soaking yourself." Mamma snatched the pitcher from Lucy's hands and slammed it back onto the tray.

Lucy looked down at the dark stain spreading over the skirt of her dress. Her hands were empty now, but she kept the glass clamped between her knees.

"It's okay, Mamma," she said. She spoke softly. She was filled with a great tenderness. "It's all mixed up with the mud now," she said. "See?" She removed the glass from between her knees, set it down on the rug beside her chair, and lifted up the skirt of her dress.

"First the mud stains, then the lemonade stains." She saw that Mamma was getting angry about something. She put her hand out and touched Mamma's arm.

"Don't get cross, Mamma," she said. "It's only my dress that's been disgraced." She began to giggle. "Did you see them out there?" she said. "Did you see the one jump in the puddle and spray me?"

The memory was enormously funny to her. Her whole

head felt enlarged with the humor of it. She let the weight of her head have the motion it craved, lolling forward in an abrupt dip that astonished her only briefly, letting the fit of laughter come all the way up to her thin shoulders, which hunched forward to protect, even as they set free, the rich comedy of it.

"Like a frog—he leapt like a frog," she said, savoring the words. "And the other one spoke like a frog. Croaked, spoked, soaked me." She looked at the soggy skirt of her dress, then laid her head on the back of the chair to laugh again. She fed the fit of laughter with the sight of Mamma, sitting up prim and proper on the sofa, her knees pressed tightly together, as though to hold up the stockings, looser than ever around her ankles, and claiming their slackness as part and parcel of the turban that had come loose and was peeling limply from Mamma's head.

"Oh, Mamma"—Lucy gasped for breath—"if only you could see yourself."

"Guttersnipes. That's what they are, a little pack of guttersnipes."

Mamma put her glass to her lips, then set it down without even sipping. Lucy bent forward, picked up her own glass from where it sat on the rug, and drank.

"They said you give them money sometimes—for ice cream." She tried to talk sensibly to cure the mad laughter that seemed to have infected her. She managed to say that clearly enough, but the feeling of nonsense lay so close to the surface that Lucy swallowed from her glass to control the smile that kept threatening her mouth.

"So, if I give them money. What else have I got to give them?" Mamma asked angrily. "Beans, rice, cornmeal? Maybe a can of meat?"

Mamma swung herself up from the sofa and marched resolutely to the kitchen. "You just come here and tell me what else have I got to give them."

Lucy followed her to the kitchen, sensing how light and graceful her body was in its movements in comparison to Mamma's. Mamma flung open the doors of the kitchen cupboards, using both hands at once. Her body swayed slightly backward with the motion of it.

"There's what I get to go on," she said bitterly, indicating the shelves. Lucy looked at the stacks of heavy polyethylene bags, propped up by large metal cans, silver and gold in color, unlabeled, stamped with large black letters that matched the legend on the plastic bags. Lucy could not read all of it; the letters seemed to run together before her eyes, blurred, came into clear focus, swam away again. She managed to pick out the words *U.S. Government, Not to Be Sold or Exchanged, For Distribution to Needy Families*.

"That's it," Mamma said, shutting the cupboard doors grimly. "Oh, I keep the peanut butter and lard in the refrigerator," she said.

"I don't get it, Mamma," Lucy said. "What is this stuff? Where does it come from?"

"It's given to me, baby. By the government. You should spend a little more time with your mother and you'd learn a lot. There's a dirty old store two blocks from here and every third Tuesday I line up with all the other social lepers and wait for them to unlock the door and give out the goodies. Oh, it's an education in itself, I tell you, to see what a regular social scale there is for outcasts.

"There's a handful of blind people go there, and they're always served first. Then come the 'ruins'—the formerly

grand who find themselves in 'reduced circumstances.' "
Mamma coughed as though there were something bitter in
her throat that had to be gotten out. Lucy closed her eyes
against the dizziness that had begun to turn her sick.

"And behind us come the mothers of families. Oh, that's
the nicest of all." Mamma let herself down onto a kitchen
chair. "I don't believe I've ever seen a one that didn't have
dirty nails or hairy legs, or the buttons off her coat. And
they always bring along the children to help them carry
things home. No shame about it, even. Just like you saw it
there on my shelf, in clear daylight, they carry those things
out onto the public streets for all the world to see that
they're on *relief*."

Mamma shook her head in disgust. "I may not have
much left, but I have my pride," she said, reaching up for
the turban that flapped loosely over her ears, ripping it off
and casting it down on the kitchen table.

"And while I'm at it, I'll roll these stockings down," she
said, reaching up under the skirt of her dress, slithering
down the hose, forming them deftly into firm, sausagelike
rolls about her ankles.

"I've still got the decency to go over there with a shop-
ping bag to put my things in," she said, her voice trembling, her lips twisting into a bitter excuse for a smile.

"Now," she said, drumming her fingers on the table,
"now do you see why I won't have you and your sister
growing up here with me? Now that you're going on to a
good home, it's time you learned what I've spared you."

She opened the refrigerator door. Lucy did not look at
her. She heard the motor click on, heard the initial rumble
that quieted to a troubled buzz, heard Mamma sliding
glass over the metal shelf. The door thudded shut and

Mamma set down a Mason jar in the center of the table. She regarded it gloomily for a moment.

"Mamma, put the ice water back," Lucy said. "I don't want any, and you might as well have your drink. I know that's what you're dying for."

"I've done all my dying, honey," Mamma said. "And it isn't ice water. It's vodka. Colorless, odorless, tasteless. And you've had enough of it already to put out the lights in a full-grown man."

Lucy watched her unscrew the cap of the jar, tilt back her head, and drink. She watched the motions of Mamma's throat swallowing, and tried to imagine a colorless, odorless, tasteless liquor. It was impossible.

"I think I have to lie down," she said thickly, lurching away from the doorframe she had been using for support, groping her way along the wall to the living room, where the red sofa loomed like a haven of final rest. Once or twice she opened her eyes to stop the room from rocking and spinning, before she fell asleep.

She woke up slowly, knowing she was not asleep, but not able to extricate herself from the thing she had been dreaming. Somehow, in the confusion of it, she had become Mamma. She let herself drift back into the dream to get the feeling again. She was the mother now; she wanted so much to do the right thing; she wanted the judge to believe her when she said she would do anything to spare her children. Cut off her arm—yes, she'd even do that if it would help—even arrange to have it bleed colorlessly, odorlessly, tastelessly. If only the judge wouldn't go away thinking badly of her. Why, she had borne the child herself. Could still remember the feeling of it. It felt a little like drowning.

Lucy opened her eyes, forced them open to verify the sensation that endured beyond the condition of dream. Dandy, the cat, lay curled embryonically on her stomach, his paws kneading against her hipbone, his large eyes narrowed to mere slits through which she could see the pupils shrunken to the size of pinpoints. She sat up, sent him sliding to the floor, where he gazed at her moodily for a moment, then opened his mouth in a wide yawning display of needlelike teeth and abrasive tongue under the hood of red corrugation that formed the roof of his mouth.

Lucy looked away from him, sheltered her head in her hands for a minute to adjust to the throbbing there. Then she went to the kitchen and washed her face in the sink. She drank from her cupped hands, trying to relieve the swollen, poisoned sensation of her mouth. The house was utterly still.

She walked back to the living room, looked out the front window, and saw, by the angle of the sun, by the presence of men in undershirts on front steps drinking beer out of quart bottles, that the afternoon was done. She had no idea where Mamma was. If she had gone to lie down herself, it would have to be in the dark back bedroom that Lucy always avoided entering. There was something nebulous and threatening about that tiny room, with its outsized furniture, its matched bed, bureau, dresser, and vanity table which held a collection of horn combs, silver-backed brushes, the ivory-cased nail buffer—all the useless tools of vanished beauty, reflected from the tilted mirror set in mother-of-pearl.

She did not even go to the door of the room to look in and see if Mamma was there. She was leaving without even saying goodbye. She knew that, but one could not say goodbye when one had not ever really said hello. She wanted no part of Mamma. The shabby pride that was an excuse for so many failures was hateful to her. The lies, the self-deceptions—it was like dressing a specter in outworn finery. She wondered, through the dull ache in her head, about what had happened here this afternoon. She wondered if Mamma had meant to do this to her, or if she had just meant to disguise, for Lucy's sake, the drinking she herself simply could not do without, even for this single afternoon.

Either way, Lucy hated her for it. And it was in anger, finally, overflowing to bitter satisfaction, that she reached into her purse for the lumpy object, unwound with infinite care the protective dressing of gauze bandages she had stolen from the infirmary at St. Michael's.

"I hope you get the message," she said in a soft, bitter voice. She had quite forgotten, as she set the crazed and mended Delft shoe back in its proper spot on the mantelpiece, that she had intended it as a gift to Mamma.

# Chapter 12

Lucy wanted to say something that would be just right before she left this afternoon, but everything she thought of was either foolish or a lie. "I'm so happy I could die," had crossed her mind several times, but that was a line from somewhere else. It had nothing to do with the sense of desolation that gnawed at the edges of her excitement. The feeling of opening a dresser drawer for a hair ribbon and coming upon bare wood, the crazy rattling of a row of empty metal hangers in her locker when she yanked open the door—"happy" was hardly the word for it. "Done" was more to the point.

She had packed the night before. The others had all surprised her, each coming forth with treasured items of apparel that, six weeks ago, it would have been worth her life to borrow for a single afternoon. "Take it," they had all insisted gruffly when she protested. Everyone seemed momentarily redeemed by the grace of Lucy's own good fortune. It was as though by pledging a special possession to her they might, in some oblique way, become a part of her success. It had come to Lucy with the suddenness of simple truth that, when she left, each one of them would have to surrender whatever part of themselves they had ever attached to her presence. When she walked out the front door this afternoon, the four left behind would not be merely the same four people minus herself. And when they missed her, if they missed her at all, it would be that part of themselves they were homesick for.

"Too bad about them," she told herself harshly, beginning to feel swamped by emotion. "Besides, they're having one fine meal today, thanks to my leaving."

The five of them were sitting around the table for their last meal together and the dinner was a festive one. Sister Gratia had been up since five o'clock, ministering to the perfection of this bird, arranging as though for a state dinner the jewel-toned melon balls, orange sections, cubes of pears and peaches, crowns of maraschino cherries that had appeared in the fruit cup of the first course. There was asparagus, so young that it tasted like something other than its usual self, swimming in a small sea of butter sauce, and in deference to the July calendar, potato salad, dressed with Sister Gratia's home-made mayonnaise. There were hot rolls and iced tea with lucent lemon slices riding on the rim of each tall glass. And on a small and elegant tea cart, brought upstairs from one of the formal reception rooms on the first floor, sat a freshly baked shortcake beside twin bowls of plump rosy strawberries and peaked sweetened cream. Poor Sister Gratia, who grumbled and complained each time she was lifted out from the pleasant twilight of fifty years ago, had completely forgotten how to speak to the girls. Her only remaining dialect was that of food, the high feast her metaphor of eloquence. The meaning of it all touched Lucy's heart.

"I bet you could just die from happiness," Carol said mournfully.

"People don't do that," Lucy said. She was chagrined to hear Carol use exactly the remark she had rejected.

"There was that saint Sister Justin read about to us. You know, the one that wanted to receive Holy Communion so much, and the first time she received, she died of ecstasy." Helen offered the example timidly.

"Ecstasy, my foot. She prayed and fasted for a month ahead of time. The little twerp probably died of hunger," Joanne said.

Ginny gave them all a dry, ironic smile. "Now *that's* something *I* could understand," she said. "If you don't carve that creature soon, I'm going to start salivating, Lucy."

Lucy censured the remark with a withering glance as she picked up the carving knife, not even thinking it strange for a seventeen-year-old girl to be deftly expert at such a skill. They had all taken turns at carving in the privileged sanctuary of their fourth-floor dining room, where unsupervised meals had been a concession to their senior status. That was before Sister Justin arrived. But today even she was honoring the privacy of the occasion.

Lucy laid slices of turkey on the serving platter beside her place, dark meat to one side, white to the other. She arranged drumsticks and heavy wing sections with geometric care, setting them out like the four points of the compass. "There," she said, putting aside her carving tools and offering the platter to Ginny, who sat at her right. She had begun to pass it to the left, realized just in time that Carol sat to her left. Carol had lifted her hands to receive the platter, her eyes imploring Lucy to invest the gesture with some significance. Lucy refused the look. She engaged her attention, instead, with Ginny, who was serving herself with generous abandon.

"Turkey's not fattening," Ginny said, half defensively. "Besides," she continued, crowding the rest of her plate with asparagus and potato salad, "I dispense with the diet for high feasts and signal occasions." She dropped her hands to her lap, waiting for the others to finish serving themselves. Her fingers patted her stomach, which was smooth and flat now, with affectionate approval, the thumbs tucked easily under the waistband of her slim denim skirt.

"You know," she said confidently, "I may be the next to leave."

"Well, get on with your plans for departure, dear," Joanne said. "I'd gladly sell any one of you into bondage for a meal like this." Her usual bland tone of mockery was strangely harsh and she stabbed at the platter of meat as though it were an enemy to her existence.

"We all thought the next going-away party was going to be yours," Helen said with mild malice, serving herself. Lucy looked up sharply, but Helen was picking dispiritedly through the carved turkey looking for dark meat. Lucy noticed how pale she was, and how thin. All of the others had deep summer tans; Helen was like a ghost at a feast of golden people.

"Helen, why is it you never get a suntan?" Lucy asked.

"I avoid the sun," Helen said. "Thin skin."

"You need a program of exposure," Ginny said. "I used to be the same. Burn and peel; then back to burning. Now I plan it out; ten minutes the first day, fifteen or twenty the second." She spoke with authority and held up her tanned forearm for evidence and approval.

"I avoid plans, too," Helen said quietly.

"Thin skin, you know," Joanne said. Everyone wanted to laugh, but no one did.

"Well, three have been served; you can begin," Lucy said, inventing the courteous observance on the spot as Carol took the turkey platter from Helen. There were not going to be any personal explosions at this last meal together, she resolved, feeling the burden of social control upon herself. The pleasant sounds of silver against china, punctuated by pleased remarks about the food, neutralized the atmosphere. Carol served herself and handed the plate to Lucy wordlessly. Lucy took it from her gratefully. It was so much easier to be a friend, she thought, when you weren't being asked to hand over a piece of yourself in exchange for half a gnawed heart that someone dropped in your lap as though it were some sort of treasure token.

"I *hope* you'll come and see me—all of you," she said suddenly. "Mrs. Wyatt said I was to feel free to invite anyone any time. She said she was going to keep reminding me that this was my home now until she saw there was no chance of my forgetting it." She recalled the remark and offered it to them with shy pride.

"What's her house like?" Helen asked.

"What is *she* like?" Ginny asked.

"Well—" Lucy finished chewing on the piece of turkey in her mouth, swallowed and sipped from her iced tea before answering. "I've never seen her house, so I can't say a thing about it, except that it's supposed to be big."

"You *are* a gambler, aren't you," Joanne said.

"What do you mean?" Lucy asked.

"Well, you say you only know it's supposed to be big. It might be a big dump, mightn't it? Rooms and rooms and rooms full of wrack and ruin. Plaster falling off in lumps right in the middle of the dining-room table. Plop. Right in the soup." Joanne shook her head in surprise and wiped imaginary soup out of her eye with the corner of her dinner napkin. They laughed briefly. Encouraged, Joanne went on. "Did you ever see some of these big old houses? Water stains on the wallpaper making faces at you all the time. Really," she insisted when Lucy opened her mouth to protest. "Little brown wrinkled faces. They usually show up in corners by the ceiling. They're great in bedrooms, peering down at you when you try to go to sleep." She screwed up her face in horrible imitation, crossing her eyes, lifting her bottom teeth out and over her upper lip, pressing the flesh of her cheeks into creases with her long thin fingers.

"I'm scared already," Lucy said dryly.

"Well, you needn't be," Joanne said between mouthfuls of food. "They don't bite." She nibbled at a roll serenely.

"I suppose that's left for the rats in the attic," Helen said. Her words, as usual, were uttered without any suggestion of color, so that Lucy could not tell if she was encouraging Joanne or attempting, in her helpless way, to defeat the conversation.

"Helen, you should know by now that I am *not* given to fantasy." Joanne narrowed her eyes to emphasize the reality of her observations. "I'm quite sure there are no rats in the attic of Lucy's new home." She spoke assertively, then cocked her head to one side as though reminded of something. "There are probably mice in the kitchen," she said tentatively, "and there are surely big black waterbugs in the basement—the kind that crunch when you step on them—" She glanced briefly toward Lucy to verify the effect of her remarks. A confusion of anger and distaste obscured every trace of Lucy's former confidence. Encouraged, Joanne allowed herself the luxury of a firm conclusive statement. "You can be certain that there are no rats in the attic."

Ginny said, "Better rats in the attic than skeletons in the closet, right, Lucy?" Ginny never stopped chattering, but her last remark rescued the conversation. Every now and then, Lucy thought, she said something decent. And at least she was good at faking cheerfulness.

The rest of the meal went smoothly. They talked quietly among themselves, walking carefully among reminiscences, selecting for conversation and remembrance only those things that were amusing or pleasant. By the end of the hour, Lucy felt healed. She stood by the tea cart, cut the cake, and ladled on whipped cream and strawberries, then presented each girl with her dessert plate. "It isn't much, but it's all I have to give," she joked, feeling, at the same time, something serious and ceremonious about bending to each of them, one by one, to offer something fine and pleasing. They all sensed that it was the end, and they lingered over dessert even though there seemed to be nothing more to say to one another. Lucy made the first move, folding her napkin carefully along the creases and pushing back her chair.

"I think I'd better start getting ready," she said quietly, standing there, feeling a spot of hot sun on the top of her hair, noticing how they all avoided meeting her eyes, wanting to fix the moment and the exact feeling of it in her mind forever. "If anybody comes looking for me, I'm downstairs with Marcella," she said, and left them.

She started downstairs, wondering that she should be breaking into perspiration as the air grew visibly cooler. She drew her index finger backward over her upper lip to dry it. "Marcella will be the hardest," she said to herself. "After Marcella, the rest will be easy."

Marcella was lying on her bed, face down, dressed in white cotton shorts and shirt, the long mane of dark hair drawn up over her head in a thick coil across the pillow. Her arms and legs were spread straight and wide apart and with the hair gave her form the outline of an almost perfect star shape. Lucy stood in the doorway for a minute, not moving, not even breathing.

"I know you're there; you know I'm here. You might as well come in." The star moved slightly at its center, then drew in its points, one by one, the dark hair coming last as Marcella gathered herself up off the bed and stood to greet Lucy. She held up one hand, palm outward, and said, "Salutations."

"Marcella." Lucy could think of nothing else to say.

"I was going to say 'Greetings,' but then I remembered that's what they say to men when they're going in the army. I think 'Salutations' is a good one for women who are going into the army, don't you?"

"It has a certain feminine ring to it," Lucy agreed. "Too bad I'm not going in the army."

"Oh, but you are," Marcella said instantly. She continued to hold up her hand like someone frozen in the motion of stopping traffic.

Lucy went up to her, covered Marcella's hand with her own, and gently curled the fingers downward into a fist, which she took in her own. "I'm going to a new home, Marcella, a foster home," she insisted quietly.

Marcella smiled at her indulgently, as though she had said something quite mad, quite impossible. "You're in the army now, you're in the army now," she began singing, marching around the dormitory, dragging Lucy, who would not let go of her hand, into the ragged, improvised march.

"Marcella, sit down with me. I want to talk to you," Lucy said. Marcella squatted down on the floor, prying back Lucy's fingers with her free hand, then stroking the released fingers as though they had suffered some possible injury. She avoided looking at Lucy. Lucy sat on the edge of Marcella's bed.

"Won't you sit here beside me?" she said.

"I'm lying low," Marcella said, shifting from squat to prone posture. "I'm not ready to join up."

"Join up?" Lucy said.

"They may draft me, but I'm not volunteering," Marcella said.

"Marcella, what's this army business all about?" Lucy asked.

"You tell me," Marcella said. "You're the one who's

going in." Lucy closed her eyes, tried to collect her thoughts and shut out the demands of sight and sound about them that were making it hard to reach Marcella. But it was impossible to talk to Marcella without looking at her. Lucy opened her eyes almost immediately. Marcella was poking her finger into the strands of a small shag rug on the floor by her bed, searching among the threads for one long enough to do something with. Failing, she brushed the pile down flat with the palm of her hand and gazed stubbornly away from Lucy for a full half minute. Suddenly she jerked her head around, the heavy hair tumbling down into her eyes. She raked it back nervously with her fingers, wiping away, with the same gesture, the tears that were swimming there.

"Go ahead and join the army," she said. "Get in there and fight for freedom." She shrank back from the hand Lucy reached out toward her. "Put on the uniform. Learn how to use a weapon; learn how to take care of it—it may save your life some day—it's your best friend." She spoke harshly, then rested her head on her arms, which were folded together into a tight cushion of flesh. She sat up abruptly. "Whatever you do," she said, speaking rapidly this time, rushing her words together, "don't think about the dead or the wounded. You'll never win a war that way. Think about what you're fighting for. Tell yourself that you're fighting to make the world a better place for everyone. For your loved ones back at home. Back at the Home." A ghost of the old smile flickered across Marcella's face at the last remark as if it had amused her. She spoke more calmly, almost reasonably. "I'm too young for war, Lucy," she said. "I wouldn't even make it as a mascot. But you be a good soldier, you hear?"

She came and sat beside Lucy on the bed, fitting herself against Lucy's shoulder, allowing herself to be held by Lucy's arm around her waist.

Lucy made herself start over again from the beginning, ignoring all that Marcella had said, telling her as if she had not already told her five or six times in the past week. "I'm going to live with some people named Mr. and Mrs. Wyatt," she said. "They're taking me to their house this afternoon. It's not very far away from here. You'll be coming to visit me there as soon as I'm settled."

Marcella nodded to show that she understood.

"I'm not really going away, Marcella," Lucy said. "I'm just going to change places, in a way. I need more room." She held Marcella closer to her with one arm while with the other she gestured toward the windows and walls that were around them. "I don't mean this kind of room," she said, struggling for the right words. "I need to get away from so many people—I need some peace and quiet and privacy so I can grow up, Marcella. Do you know what I mean?"

"I make my own peace and quiet and privacy," Marcella said, without reproach, "but I know what you mean."

"You can come to see me there—and I can come to see you here," Lucy said. She felt herself choking on breath, needing to get it all said while she had the chance.

"Every day?" Marcella said with urgency.

"Oh, Marcella, not every day. I don't see you every day here, you know that."

"I don't need to see you every day when I know I can if I have to," Marcella said stubbornly. Lucy could feel her tightening inside the tiny armor of skin. She felt Marcella slipping away, joggled her gently back, not letting go for an instant.

"I'll make you a promise," she said. "Any time you know you have to see me, you just phone me. I'll come. No matter what, I'll come."

Marcella looked up, her face working to adjust from doubt to this sudden possibility of hope. She caught at Lucy's hand, turned it palm upward in her lap, and traced tenderly along the lines there as though to discover, or leave, a message.

"You've never broken a promise to me in my life," she said softly, more to herself than to Lucy.

Lucy seized on the remark. She took her arm from around Marcella's waist, put both her hands on Marcella's shoulders, and drew her squarely face to face with her own gaze. Her eyes would not let go. She waited until she was certain Marcella was waiting to hear what she would say. Then she poured out her words carefully, slowly, feeling her hands on Marcella's shoulders tremble as though they were responsible for bearing safely to Marcella a beaker, full to the brim, of something sacred, precious and life-giving.

"I will never break a promise to you," she said steadily. "I will always come when you call me. Marcella, I'll walk through fire and flood just to hold your hand if that's what you need."

Marcella's face was touched with glory; the beauty, the sheer miracle of her smile blessed and burned at Lucy's heart. Nowhere else on earth was there a person, never a single one since time's beginning, who could smile like that, saying everything in a moment without a word. Lucy bore the length of that smile, not interrupting it, not defending herself against it, taking the imprint of it somewhere inside herself. Marcella was the first to speak, but all she said was, "Oh Lucy, oh Lucy, I do love you."

"Will you come downstairs with me after I've dressed?" Lucy asked her finally. "Would you like to meet Mr. and Mrs. Wyatt?"

Marcella shook her head slowly. "Not today," she said, "but soon. You look very pretty today, Lucy," she said. "I think maybe you look beautiful." She cocked her head to the side and studied Lucy carefully. "You *are* beautiful today," she said finally with conviction, "but I think maybe it's just for me. I don't want to come downstairs with everybody else and watch it all run out over the edges. Too many edges can do that," she said when she saw Lucy beginning to smile. "And besides, they'll all be saying goodbye. *I'm* not saying goodbye, am I, Lucy?" she asked.

"No, Marcella," Lucy said.

"Okay, then. You run and get dressed now. And I'll see you soon. As soon as I need to. Right?"

"Right," Lucy answered, but she felt somehow as though a stone were being rolled against her heart. She was exhausted by her conversation with Marcella. She was not used to such heady talk. Walking through fire and flood was not her style of activity, she thought wryly to herself, feeling her knees tremble as she stood up from the bed. Even the taste of the words on her tongue had been strange and painful. "But I meant it," she told herself, turning to Marcella for a last look, a last aching moment that lifted her arms, without their own consent, to hold Marcella against her in an embrace that lasted longer than she wanted it to.

"Wish me luck," she whispered, breaking away.

"I wish it," Marcella said, smiling, pushing her softly, like a toy that needs to be started on its performance, into the short walk to the door. Lucy was almost out of the dormitory when Marcella called to her. She turned, looked across the small forest of beds that separated them, into what seemed to have become the small canyons of Marcella's deep smiling eyes.

"Lucy, don't forget what General Sherman said."

"What's that?" Lucy asked.

"War is hell," Marcella answered, calling out the words in a high, thin voice that floated into the air both of them were unconsciously breathing.

She had expected the rest to be fairly mechanical. There was nothing to do but change her dress into the clean one that was hanging, strangely alone, in her emptied locker, then wait by the window until she saw the Wyatts driving up, go downstairs with her two suitcases and say goodbye to Sister Christine. Then she would be on her way. She was surprised to find the other four grouped around her bed, talking quietly, obviously waiting for her, each with an odd-shaped parcel in her hands.

"Beware of freaks bearing gifts," Joanne said, dropping her small packet onto Lucy's bed. Lucy sat down, smiled with pleased embarrassment at all of them, and began to fumble with the thin red ribbon that held the white tissue-paper wrapping together.

"I don't know why you're doing this," she said in confusion to hide how touched she was.

"Neither do we, really," Joanne said. "Hurry up and open it."

Lucy tore at the wrappings and three small bottles of nail polish fell out, one red, one pink, one bright orange. She felt herself blushing.

"Are you making fun of me?" she asked, making fists of her hands to hide her bitten nails.

"Don't be an idiot," Joanne said. "Those are a promise to the future. You're going to stop biting your nails now that we're not around to worry you to death." She spoke assertively, picked up the bottles, ribbon, and torn wrapping herself, and snapped open the locks on one of the suitcases on Lucy's bed, dropping it all onto the top of the folded clothes there. "Come on, there's three more presents," she said impatiently, cutting short Lucy's thanks.

"For you," Ginny said simply, handing her package next. Lucy undid the ribbon, folded back the tissue carefully this time, and sat staring with disbelief at the bright red, white, and blue stripes of Ginny's new bathing suit. "Oh, you *can't* give this to me, Ginny," she protested. "I couldn't possibly wear your brand-new suit—I just won't take it." Lucy could feel a lump rising in her throat.

"Yes, you can wear it—that's what's so neat about it. *You* wearing *my* bathing suit. I *want* you to have it," Ginny insisted simply. "Don't worry, I'll get another one," she said.

"I won't get another one of these, but don't you say to me what you said to Ginny about not taking it," Carol said quietly, handing her package to Lucy with her hands seeming not to let go. "I want you to remember me," she said.

"I will remember you, Carol; I'll always remember you," Lucy said, knowing, before she even opened it, from the faint odor of mothballs and lavender sachet, that Carol had given up her blue cashmere sweater.

Helen's package, like Helen herself, was thin and untidy. Wherever the four of them had managed to rummage up the tissue paper and red ribbon, they had managed to run out of it before Helen wrapped her gift. Even so, Lucy could not make out what it might be that had no real shape, no dimension to it under the single sheet of tissue fastened clumsily together with plain Scotch tape. She felt almost afraid to open it; afraid to spoil the magic that each gift had carried about itself so far. Each of the girls had managed, out of their small store of possessions, to give Lucy the thing that spoke most eloquently to her about themselves. Lucy wished now that she had opened Helen's first. It would have been better that way. Helen stood by, impassive, pale, and when Lucy looked at her she blinked her eyes, which looked red and watery—like a chicken's, Lucy thought—but she said nothing. Lucy peeled back the tape, fussing with it longer than was necessary. The tissue tore under its small burden, and into Lucy's lap there tumbled a single, wrinkled, soiled rectangle of heavy material, bearing in fine stitches the completed sampler motto: *Hours fly, Flowers die. New Days, New Ways Pass by. Love stays.*

Lucy began to cry then. Not the easy tears of sentiment, but deep sobs that cut their way through her like blades of breath, coming from some place in herself she had not known about. She covered her face with her hands, feeling its expression twisted out of shape, feeling the dreadful poverty of their existences—her own as well as the others—in the giving and receiving of the gifts. It took her a few minutes, in which none of them said a word, to chain back the sudden creatures that had been loosed upon her heart. Finally she was just a girl full of tears saying goodbye to her friends, laughing and crying at the same time as she looked for something to wipe her eyes and blow her nose on, taking the box of Kleenex that someone handed her, and finally getting up, putting the small parcels into her suitcase, and saying, "If I don't change my dress, the Wyatts will think they've gotten Little Orphan Annie by mistake."

She had meant to linger over her leave-taking of the house, fixing in her memory each arch, window, and hallway exactly as they would look this last time. But there was no time for that. Before she had finished dressing, Ginny, stationed at the window, called out, "They're here, Lucy." Joanne and Helen each picked up a suitcase, and Carol, with one deep sigh, said, "I'm coming to the front door with you."

Sister Justin and Sister Christine were in the front hall with the Wyatts. Somewhere in the back of her mind Lucy heard the murmur of astonished approval from the other four when they first saw Mrs. Wyatt. She had seen, out of the corner of her eye, the curious faces of younger girls crowding in corridors and doorways to stare at her as at a celebrity as she made her way down to the first floor, but it was all nebulous, dreamlike. She felt, with a kind of physical shock, Sister Justin's hand on her arm.

"Come to the chapel, and say goodbye to the dear Lord," she whispered, turning Lucy away before she had a chance to do anything but throw a tremulous smile toward Mr. and Mrs. Wyatt. Lucy let herself be led to the chapel, wondering why Sister whispered as though this were a hospital corridor or a funeral parlor. She knelt down in the last pew and folded her hands. But she could not pray. She could only think, with strange wonder in her heart, "I'm leaving the Home today—right now." Sister Justin tapped her on the shoulder and said, "You'd better come now, Lucy." Lucy slid out of the pew, genuflected, dipped her hand in the holy water font, and traced the sign of the cross onto her shoulders. Sister Christine walked down the hall to meet her.

"Are you ready to leave us, Lucy?" she asked.

"I think so, Sister," Lucy said in a small voice.

"Then we won't stand around talking about it," Sister said firmly. "You'll be back to visit us," Sister Christine said in a matter-of-fact voice that somehow made everything easier. "And I suspect some of us will be visiting you." She inclined her glance to the small delegation of girls who were suddenly stopped in the conversation they had begun with the Wyatts.

"I'm giving you a lovely girl; take good care of her," Sister Christine said to the Wyatts. In their answering rush of assurances, she turned to Lucy and took her in her arms, suddenly, warmly, holding her in the strangely fleshed and bodied sense of a close embrace.

"Goodbye, dear little one," she said with unaccustomed tenderness, "and God be with you." She held Lucy off at arm's length, smiled at her, then turned away for a moment, almost with annoyance, to wipe at her eyes. Lucy's own eyes were as grainy as dust. She supposed she had run them dry earlier. She could sense the beating of her heart; it seemed larger than usual. She took a deep breath over the sudden feeling of it, saw that Mr. Wyatt had her bags and that Mrs. Wyatt was waiting to take her out the front door. She had a final look at them all standing there to see